SECRET, SILENT
SCREAMS

SECRET, SILENT SCREAMS

Joan Lowery Nixon

Delacorte
Press

Published by
Delacorte Press
The Bantam Doubleday Dell Publishing Group, Inc.
666 Fifth Avenue
New York, New York 10103

Library of Congress Cataloging in Publication Data

Nixon, Joan Lowery.
    Secret, Silent screams.

    Summary: A high school senior is convinced her friend Barry
did not commit suicide but was a murder victim, and she
endangers her own life to prove it.
    [1. Mystery and detective stories.   2. Suicide—Fiction]
I. Title.
PZ7.N65Sh   1988   [Fic]   88-417
ISBN 0-440-50059-1

Manufactured in the United States of America

October 1988

10 9 8 7 6 5 4 3 2 1

BG

*This book is for you
because you are unique and important and special.
Hang on to your dreams.
Hold tight to hope.
Someone rejoices in your joy.
Someone cares about your sorrows and your fears.
I do, too.
I care.*

SECRET, SILENT
SCREAMS

CHAPTER • 1

Marti Lewis shivered as she opened the door to the Farrington Park police station. Her stomach ached, and she fought back the nausea that burned her throat. *I made the decision. I have to stick with it,* she repeated over and over to herself. *I haven't got a choice.* She glanced down at the dark cotton dress she had worn since early that morning. There was a smudge near the hem of the skirt. Maybe she should go home and change. Yes, and wear something that would look more—more businesslike.

No. She had to be here. Now.

Marti paused, clinging to the edge of the door with numb fingers, and surveyed the small room with its row of empty desks. The only occupant was a young woman with short, curly red hair who was dressed in a pale blue short-sleeved blouse. She was bent over some papers on a desk at the far end of the room, so intent on what she

1

was writing that she didn't look up. Marti tried to speak, but the only sound that come from her mouth was a slight, raspy cough.

Startled, the woman sat up and put down her pen. "May I do something for you?" she asked.

Marti hesitated, wanting to turn and run, but she slowly shut the door and walked toward the woman's desk. Twice she cleared her throat before she was able to speak.

"I-I need—I want to talk to a policeman."

"I'm a police officer," the woman answered.

"But you're—"

"—a woman." Her dry tone as she finished the sentence embarrassed Marti.

"That's not what I meant." Marti shook her head so vigorously that her pale blond hair swung in front of her eyes, and she had to sweep it back. "You don't understand. It's just that you're very young, and I need someone who can help me to . . . who can help me." Tears puddled her eyes and she rubbed the tears away, furious at herself for giving in to them.

The woman stood and firmly extended her right hand. As Marti took it, the woman said, "Thanks for the compliment. I'll take it as that. I'm Officer Karen Prescott. And you?"

"Marti Lewis."

Karen dropped Marti's hand and gestured toward a nearby chair, saying, "Please sit down, Marti, and tell me your problem. I'll do my best to help you. That's why I'm here."

Marti, still tensed for flight, slid stiffly onto the hard wooden chair and gripped the edge of the officer's desk. "This is the first time I've been in a police station," Marti said. She glanced around the room again. "I

2

thought there would be a lot of policemen here. Like there are in some of the shows on TV. You know—with all sorts of people going back and forth." Marti knew that everything she was babbling sounded stupid, but she couldn't stop the flow of words. "There isn't even a secretary. At first, I thought you were a secretary, but then . . . oh, I could see that patch on your shirt. I guess you don't call it that. It's an emblem, right? Or whatever. You know—that design that shows you're an officer. I mean, this isn't a very busy place. The phone isn't ringing. I thought the phone would keep ringing."

Karen smiled, leaned back in her chair, and interrupted. "Relax, Marti. If it will make you feel better, let me assure you that we do have a secretary. Her name is Alice, and she took some time off to go to the dentist. Our chief's on vacation; the sergeant and his partner are out on patrol; and we have other officers who are working different shifts." She held out her arms toward the quiet room. "We don't need a large staff. Farrington Park is not a very large city."

Marti nodded in agreement with that last statement. She had lived in Houston, a large city, when she was younger, before her parents had fallen in love with Farrington Park, which was designed from the start to be a model city.

"Even if it takes longer to commute to our jobs, it's worth it, Josh," Marti's mother had said as the three of them had driven up and down the gently curved streets, with their open-house signs in front of model homes, town houses, and apartments. She had tucked in a strand of her always tidy blond hair, and her words bubbled over each other as she added, "Wait till you see the mall. It's beautiful! And the country club! Oh, Josh, you're going to love the Olympic-sized pool and the beautiful tennis courts. And we're not far from I-10. We can take it right into downtown Houston."

"There *is* that question of timing," Marti's father had said. "I don't think we should make a decision until we've driven the route in rush-hour traffic."

Marti understood her father well enough to recognize the pros-and-cons game he was playing with her mother, and she knew he was sold on the idea of moving to Farrington Park.

"The move will be good for Marti," her mother said, with a smiling glance toward the backseat. "It will be so much safer than living in the city, and the high school's designed on something they call a flow plan, which I don't understand completely, but Jeannie Evans said it's the very latest thing."

No one had asked Marti how she felt about the move, and since she was only in the fifth grade, she couldn't have cared less about high-school flow plans; but ever since she found out that her best friend, Kim Roberts, was going to move to Farrington Park, she was content that her parents wanted to live there too.

Marti had adapted quickly to their big house with the large bedrooms and paneled den with double sliding glass-doors overlooking a landscaped patio. Sometimes, though, while she was working in school or on the swim team or in ballet class, she thought about the house and felt a little sorry for it—and for most of the other houses in Farrington Park—because they stood empty every day, their windows like huge glass eyes searching for their owners. It wasn't until evening, when all the parents were home from their jobs in Houston, and there was a scramble of dinner preparations and homework and television and baths and bed, that the houses could feel filled and content.

4

"Poor house," Marti had once said aloud, and explained her feelings in answer to her mother's surprised question.

But her mother had laughed and rolled her eyes at Marti's father. "Oh, Marti, my love," she said. "You have such a wild imagination!"

"Well? What's the problem?" Karen's question jolted Marti back to the present.

Marti cleared her throat again, gulped in a deep breath, and took a firmer grip on the edge of the desk. She frowned as she studied the police officer's carrot-red hair and freckled upturned nose. "How long have you been a police officer?" she asked.

"Three years, most of them spent in Houston. I came to Farrington Park about two months ago.

"How old *are* you?" Marti demanded.

The woman shrugged. "Twenty-four," she said. "Does it make a difference?"

"Well, I told you," Marti began, then slumped a little, the defensive stiffness dissolving from her backbone, "I have to talk to someone about something serious."

"How serious?"

"Murder," Marti said, and felt the blood drain from her face.

"Put your head down if you feel faint." Marti was aware that the officer had leapt from her chair and sprinted to the soft-drink machine in the corner.

"I don't feel faint," Marti insisted as she fought against the black spots that swam in front of her eyes. But she took a long drink from the icy can that was thrust into her hand, and she let the drops of moisture drip down her fingers into her palm and run down her arm.

Karen hitched her chair a little closer to Marti's and leaned forward. "Better now?"

"Yes. Thanks." Marti took another long swallow of the soft drink.

"Okay, Marti," Karen said, her eyes narrowed and probing, "Tell me your story. What do you know about a murder?"

Marti put down the soft-drink can and once again gripped the edge of the desk. "Barry Logan is—was—my friend. His funeral was this morning," she said. "The police said he committed suicide and everyone believes it, but I know Barry didn't kill himself."

Karen's lips parted as though she were going to speak, but Marti rushed ahead. "Listen to me. I know. Barry and I have been good friends since sixth grade, and now we're—were—high-school seniors. We live—lived—next door to each other, and we've made so many plans together."

Karen placed a hand on top of Marti's and murmured, "It's hard to lose a friend. I'm very sorry."

"That's all everyone says," Marti answered. "Being sorry isn't enough. You have to find out who murdered Barry." A tear rolled down her cheek, and she impatiently brushed it away.

"When someone's been terribly hurt it's hard to think clearly. It's hard to accept what happened," Karen said. "If we talk about Barry's suicide—"

"His murder!"

Karen took a long breath. "If we talk about this, it's going to be extremely difficult for you."

"I know that." Marti sat up a little straighter, her chin jutting out with determination. "But I have to tell the police what I know, and you're the only officer here. Officer—uh, Prescott, did you say?"

"That's right. Karen Prescott."

"Do I call you Officer Prescott? Or Ms. Prescott?" Marti gulped down a sob that threatened to explode in her throat. "I want to do this the right way. I want you to really listen to me."

Karen's voice softened. "Take it easy, Marti. We don't need any formalities. Call me Karen if it makes it easier for you."

Marti nodded. "Okay. Karen." She sniffled loudly. "You'll listen to me?"

"Of course I will."

Karen handed her a box of tissues that was on the corner of the desk, and Marti wiped her eyes and blew her nose. "I'm ready to talk right now," Marti said, "because the longer we wait, the harder it will be to catch Barry's murderer. Isn't that right? Aren't you supposed to find clues and evidence as soon as possible?"

Karen sidestepped the question. "Have you discussed this with your parents?" she asked.

Marti shuddered. "My parents. Yes, I did, and of course they told me I'm wrong. My mother offered me one of her tranquilizers. So I came here to talk to someone who would listen and who could do something about it." She tried to stop her lower lip from quivering as she added, "It's important to me that people know the truth because Barry was my friend."

"Have you thought that your friendship for Barry might be keeping you from admitting the truth to yourself?"

Marti sighed. "Do you have a brother?"

"No."

"Well, then, a guy who's a really good friend? Maybe someone you love?"

7

"I—yes. I guess so."

"Then you know that when you really care about someone you begin to learn how he thinks and feels until it's almost like you were thinking and feeling with him."

Karen's eyes dropped, and her cheeks flushed. She picked up a pencil, rubbing it and studying it as though it were the most important item on her desk. Finally she looked up, and her eyes met Marti's. "There is—was —someone like that," she said. "If what happened to Barry had happened to him, I admit that I wouldn't have wanted to believe it either. But we have to face the facts. Last May, just before graduation, two of the seniors at Farrington Park High committed suicide. Do you remember?"

"Of course I remember. They were in the class ahead of ours, but I knew them. They'd been dating for two years, and then they broke up. Robin still loved Al, so she couldn't take it. Then Al blamed himself and he—"

Karen held up a hand, interrupting her. "Barry was one of Al's friends, wasn't he?"

"Barry was just about everybody's friend."

"But one of Al's particular friends?"

"Not a close friend," Marti said. "They were on the tennis team together, and they both had part-time jobs at Jumbo Burger, but it wasn't a strong friendship like the Cuatros'."

"What are the Cuatros?"

"It's a special group Barry was in. The guys were all taking Spanish together in junior high, and since there were four of them, they named themselves the Cuatros."

"They remained close friends?"

"Yes."

"Was Al in this group?"

"No." Marti shook her head impatiently. "There was Barry and Charlie Villeret and Tony Lopez."

"That's only three. *Cuatro* means four, doesn't it?"

Marti hesitated for just an instant. "I forgot about Thad Miller. He was the fourth one, but he doesn't live here anymore." She looked at the desk, then back to Karen. "Don't you need to write down what I tell you? Or get out Barry's file? Or something?"

"You've been watching too many cop shows on TV," Karen said. "We did make up a file on Barry, but I don't have to pull it. I remember the information that came in. There wasn't much. The tennis coach told Bill— Sergeant Nieman—that Barry was upset about Al's death, that he didn't get over it right away."

Marti nodded reluctantly. "Sure, Barry was upset at the time. And I know what Barry told the coach because he told me too. Barry always talked to me about how he felt. He wondered if maybe he could have helped Al so that he wouldn't have killed himself. The night before Al—before it happened—Al had called Barry, but Barry wasn't home. He was working at Jumbo Burger, so Barry's dad took the message. It was late when Barry got in and his dad was asleep, so he didn't tell Barry that Al had called until the next morning. By then it was too late."

"Are you saying that Barry blamed himself?"

"No. He knew it wasn't his fault. At first he wondered if he could have helped Al if he'd just been home to talk to him, and he was kind of surprised that Al had called him, because their friendship wasn't that close. Then Barry found out that Al had called some other guys, too, and most of them weren't home either, so Al must have just been going down a list he had in his mind, looking

9

for someone to talk to." Marti sighed. "Barry didn't blame himself."

"It may have upset him more than you know. If he—"

"It upset all of us!" Marti got to her feet and walked the length of the room and back. She leaned on the desk and said, "The suicides shook us all up. It's scary, you know? Like you can't believe it really happened. Like maybe you could run the tape over again and Robin and Al would be back at school, and the whole thing would be a bad dream that went away."

Karen pursed her lips as she thought. "I remember Sergeant Nieman mentioning Barry's parents. They told him that they hadn't noticed at the time, but looking back at the situation, it was possible that Barry had shown signs of being withdrawn or moody."

"How would they know?" Marti exploded. "They were hardly ever with him! Barry was *never* withdrawn or moody!" She turned away from the desk and began to pace.

"Come back and sit down," Karen invited. "I'm trying to think of how to help you."

"I told you—"

"Sit down. We can't talk if you're going to pace like that. I'll get the file, and we'll go over every fact, one by one. Will that satisfy you?"

Marti didn't answer, but she walked back to her chair and perched on the edge of it, waiting until Karen returned.

Karen opened the folder and studied the top page before she looked up at Marti and said, "Just before Robin committed suicide she had been playing the tape *Sudden Death* by Flesh. It was found in the VCR."

Marti winced but didn't say a word, and Karen continued. "Apparently Al had been playing the cassette of

'Sudden Death' in his car when he crashed it at approximately ninety miles an hour into a brick wall."

"I know," Marti whispered.

"When Barry's body was found in the den by his parents at six o'clock Monday night, they discovered that he had been playing the videotape of *Sudden Death*. It was still in the VCR."

"He hated Flesh," Marti said. "He never listened to their music. And he thought *Sudden Death* was stupid. He wouldn't have played it."

Karen leaned forward intently. "Listen to the facts," she said. "The tape was there."

"Someone else must have put it there."

Karen sighed. "There was a note. It was in Barry's handwriting."

"Are you sure it was his handwriting?"

"A handwriting analyst with the Houston crime lab checked it out. He was positive. Do you know about the note?"

Marti closed her eyes against the pain. Of course she knew about the note and what it said. It had been quoted on the front page of the Houston newspapers. In a whisper she repeated, " 'The thought of suicide is a great consolation.' " Her eyelids snapped open. "Barry wouldn't have written that. It's not the way he talked or thought."

"Marti, be reasonable," Karen said. "Keep an open mind."

"I am."

"Barry shot himself with a Rossi .22 handgun. He shot himself in the right side of the head."

Marti jumped to her feet, her fingers twisted together and pressed tightly against her chest. It was even harder to fight off the burning tears, but she man-

11

aged to get her voice under control. "See? That's what I mean," she said. "You might not believe me about the music and the note, but you have to believe this. Barry didn't shoot himself."

"But his fingerprints were the only ones on the gun, and powder burns were on his right hand."

"That's it!" Marti cried, and in her intensity she reached across the corner of the desk and clutched both of Karen's hands. "He couldn't! He wouldn't have shot himself like that! Barry was *left-handed!*"

CHAPTER • 2

Marti walked home, the low September sun a deep red splash, simmering in its own smoldering heat waves. Sweat plastered the dress to her back, and the humidity caused her hair to frizz out in puffs around her face.

Barry had liked to tease her about her hair. "It looks like cotton candy," he had said the summer before they began seventh grade. "I'd like it even better if it was pink."

He had bought a packet of some kind of dye, and together they had turned her hair into a fluffy pink cloud. It was later, after Marti's mother had finally finished a long and horrified complaint of "What will people think!" that they found it was a kind of dye that wouldn't easily wash out. Marti really hadn't minded. While it lasted she liked the pink hair. It made her feel different and special, and in spite of the fact that a few people pointed and snickered, Barry had told her she looked terrific.

Barry.

Marti angrily kicked at a pebble that lay on the sidewalk. It had taken all the courage she had to go to the police for help and pour out the truth about Barry, but that officer—Karen—had studied her for a few minutes as though she could see all the way through to Marti's brain, and said only, "I'll give this some thought." That was a favorite statement for adults who wanted to stall, to get you off their backs. They'd make you wait forever for the answer, which always turned out to be "no." Marti had no illusions that Karen would help.

As she turned into Castle Lake Drive she saw two cars parked in front of the Logans' house. She supposed that people would have come and gone all through the day. Marti and her mother had visited with Mr. and Mrs. Logan after the funeral. Mom had stayed to help with the food—taking a day off from her accountant's job—and had sent Marti on to school. But Marti hadn't gone back to school with the others in Barry's class who'd been excused to attend the funeral. She had gone to the police station instead.

Impulsively, she turned into the walkway leading to the Logans' front door, pausing at the landscaped entryway as the door opened and two couples came out murmuring comforting words, hugging and patting Mrs. Logan as they said their good-byes.

Mrs. Logan—small-boned, trim, and not a bit like Barry—beckoned to Marti. "I'm so glad you came back, dear," she said. "It was a beautiful service, wasn't it? And all Barry's friends—how nice of them to be there."

Marti gulped through the tight ache in her throat and

followed Mrs. Logan into the living room, sitting down opposite her on the matching blue love seats. She tried not to look at the shuttered doors that closed off the den.

"Would you like something to eat?" Mrs. Logan went on. "Everyone's brought so much food. There's sliced ham and—oh, yes—a bowl of that orange-pineapple gelatin salad you like so much. Most of it's been put in the refrigerator, but you know where everything is in the kitchen, so you can help yourself."

Marti shook her head. "I'm really not hungry, Mrs. Logan. I just hoped that maybe we could talk." She shrugged, feeling even more miserable. "I know that you've been talking to people all day and you're probably tired, but if you wouldn't mind listening to me for just a few minutes I'd—"

Mr. Logan came into the living room from the hall that extended to the bedrooms, saying, "You were right, Alice. The nap helped." He was tall and muscular and deeply tanned from his almost daily exercise on the golf course—so much like Barry that it hurt Marti to look at him. He spotted Marti and his eyes widened. "I'm so used to seeing you sitting there that it's like it . . . it hadn't happened," he said. He sat down next to his wife, his shoulders suddenly rounding and slumped like those of an old man, and she took his hand, squeezing it gently.

"Did Barry tell you, Marti?" Mr. Logan said. "The day before—before he—died, he received a letter from A & M. He made early acceptance."

Marti nodded. "He called me right away."

"He was so proud of making the early list."

"I'm sorry about Barry," Marti whispered. "He was one of my best friends. I miss him terribly."

15

"Yes, yes. We all miss him," Mr. Logan mumbled.

But Mrs. Logan closed her eyes and said, "Forgive us, Marti. It's our fault that Barry died. The doctor and the police asked if we'd recognized the signs, and we hadn't. We should have recognized the signs."

"It's *not* your fault." Marti leaned toward them, her elbows resting on her knees. "There were no signs . . . because Barry *didn't* commit suicide. I went to the police this afternoon and told them."

They didn't react positively, as Marti had hoped. Mr. Logan's face twisted in pain, and Mrs. Logan murmured, "Oh, dear. You shouldn't have done that. What good could it do?"

"I hoped the police could find out what really happened to Barry. I know he didn't kill himself."

Mrs. Logan whimpered, and Mr. Logan absentmindedly stroked his wife's hand. "Marti," he said, "don't try for the impossible. It only makes it harder for you."

"But wouldn't you rather know that Barry hadn't taken his own life?"

Mrs. Logan began to cry, and she spoke through her tears as though she didn't know they were there. "We failed Barry in some way. We don't even know how or why. He didn't come to us. He didn't talk things over with us. We didn't even have a chance to help him."

"It wasn't like that—" Marti began.

"It's going to haunt us forever," Mrs. Logan said. "I go past his room, and I think about . . . I remember . . . I . . . how could he have done this to himself? To us?"

"He didn't!" Marti insisted. "If someone would just listen to me—"

Mr. Logan managed to struggle to his feet. "Marti,"

he said wearily, "you must be hungry. There's a lot of food left. The refrigerator is full. Why don't you get a plate and help yourself?"

"I know Barry didn't commit suicide!"

"Paul," Mrs. Logan said, "we'll have to sell this house. I can't bear living here after—"

"Thank you for coming, Marti. If you'd just go now . . ." Mr. Logan's voice was as raw and rough as if it had been rubbed across a metal grater.

"I didn't mean to hurt you," Marti stammered, fighting against the frustration and pain that welled in her throat and threatened to choke her. "I'm sorry. I thought you'd believe, as I do, that Barry wouldn't give up. He knew there was so much to live for. He wouldn't have—"

Mr. Logan placed a hand on her arm. "It's all right," he said. "We understand. You mean well. It's hard for us to accept too."

As Mrs. Logan burrowed her head against the arm of the love seat and began to sob loudly, the way a child would cry, Marti ran from the house and raced across the lawn to her own home, hiding away in her ruffled rose and white bedroom until her own tears were spent. She'd made everything worse for the Logans, and she hadn't meant to. Why wouldn't anyone believe her?

She sat cross-legged on the bed, trying to think. Maybe she could get some help from Barry's friends— maybe one or more of the remaining Cuatros. She could picture the four of them—so often together. Charlie was the tallest and stockiest, with a thick shock of dark brown hair. He looked older than the others, even though he was the youngest by two months. Tony, black-eyed and good-looking, was the shortest but made up for it by working out until he had muscles all the guys envied. Thad was thin, with olive-green eyes and dark blond hair. He smiled a lot, but his smile had always made Marti uncomfortable. And Barry, with his sandy hair and deep blue eyes that crinkled with laugh lines at the corners . . . Barry was handsome and bright and full of fun and—

Marti rolled over on her stomach and squirmed across the quilt until she could reach the telephone and her address book. She looked up Charlie Villeret's phone number and dialed.

When Charlie answered she told him bluntly much of what she had told Officer Prescott.

After she had finished, the line was silent for a few moments as though Charlie had clapped his hand over the mouthpiece. When he spoke she could hear the tears in his voice. "Hey, Marti," he said, "we all feel the same way. It's hard to take. But don't jump off like that. You sound kind of weird."

"But didn't you hear me? I told you—"

"I know what you told me." He was obviously trying to be patient. "Look. You say that someone murdered Barry."

"That's right."

"Okay, then. Who?"

"Who? That's what I don't know."

"Think about it. Barry didn't have any enemies. Who'd kill him and try to make it look like a suicide? One of us? One of his friends?"

"No. Of course not," Marti stammered.

Charlie let out a long sigh. "Then forget it. Please. Just forget all this, and let it be over."

"Forget it? Every time you remember Barry do you

want to think of him as someone who took his own life and hurt everybody who loved him?"

There was a gasp, then silence. Finally Charlie said, "That's not fair."

"Will you help me?"

"There's nothing I can do."

"Yes, there is," Marti said. "You can answer some questions for me."

"The police already asked me questions. I've told them everything I knew."

"Charlie, I need to find out everything I can about Barry and how he was feeling and what he was thinking."

Charlie groaned. "Not now, Marti. I don't want to talk about Barry now." The line went dead.

Marti dialed Tony's number next. After she had told him what she'd told Charlie, Tony just snapped, "You're crazy!"

"I need you and Charlie to help me."

"Give it up," Tony said. "You're just going to drag everything out and make it a lot worse for everybody."

"I want to ask you some questions," she said.

"Forget it!" Marti winced at the sound of the receiver being slammed into place.

She wearily climbed from the bed and leaned against the frame of her bedroom window. Light from the arc lamps on the street outlined the Logan house. There were lights within the house too, the kitchen light spilling into long rectangles across the lawn. Directly across from her upstairs room was the dark, covered glass of Barry's bedroom window.

When they were young, they had sent each other flashlight signals and secret messages through their bedroom windows, and one summer—in an attempt to try a circus tightrope act—they had a strung a rope between the two houses, tying it securely to their bedposts. Barry had gone first. With his weight on the rope, her bed had scraped across the floor, slamming into the wall, leaving Barry hanging on to the sagging rope. He yelled at the top of his lungs until she could drag her father's double ladder from the garage to help him down. When their parents had come home from work that night, each set asking, "Did you have a nice day?" Marti and Barry had answered, "Yes," finding no reason to mention their failed tightrope act.

Marti leaned her head against the frame and closed her eyes to keep back the hot and painful tears. She had known Barry even better than she knew Kim. He'd been an everyday part of her life. They'd shared, they'd fought, they'd confided in each other. She'd been wary of whom he dated, not hesitating to make blunt comments about a couple of the girls; and he'd responded in kind, sometimes behaving like an obnoxious big brother.

She lightly touched the tip of one finger to her lips as she remembered that her first kiss had been from Barry. But aside from a few tentative, playful moments, there had been no romance between them. At the back of her mind Marti had almost expected that when they were older, when they were ready for something real, she and Barry would find each other.

Now it was too late.

"Marti!" her mother called from the foot of the stairs. "Kim's here."

Marti ran to throw open the door and shout down, "Kim! Come on up!" If anyone would listen and understand, it would be Kim.

Kim, who was as short as Marti was tall, as dark-

haired as Marti was blonde, ran up the stairs and
wrapped her friend in a clumsy hug. Kim, who'd been
discouraged politely from ever attending another ballet class and who'd been kicked off the swim team, had
kept trying to find her niche until she happily landed on
the Yearbook staff. She never allowed anything to dis-
rupt her good-natured outlook on life, and all her bub-
bling optimism seemed to spill over on those around
her.

Marti badly needed to talk to Kim. She sat on the
floor opposite Kim, her back to the window so she
couldn't see Barry's house, and told Kim everything she
had thought and done and said about Barry's death.

But Kim's look was one of pity as she answered,
"Marti, the police called it a suicide. This is their business. They know what they're doing."

The tight knot in Marti's chest grew more painful. "I
thought you'd help me."

"Of course I'll help you. Whatever you want. Just tell
me, and I'll do it."

"But you don't believe me," Marti murmured.

Kim looked down at her hands, and her voice was a
bare whisper. "I'm sorry, Marti," she said. "I can't. I
don't."

Marti hadn't wanted to go to class the next morning,
but her mother had said, "You have to pick up where
you left off. The world keeps going on, and you have to
go with it."

"Those are clichés," Marti muttered, aware that she
was unreasonably angry that her mother looked the
way she always did, so dully neat and businesslike and
unperturbed in her cool gray jacket and skirt, a perfectly tied black bow at the neck of her white blouse. It

21

wasn't fair that the world went on as though nothing had happened.

Mom had simply shrugged, her palms held outward helplessly, and Marti could see her own pain reflected in her mother's eyes. "It's the only way I know how to say it," Mom said. "It's hard to talk about death. The words always sound all wrong and fake, as though they were copied from those awful sentimental greeting cards. I'm sorry, Marti. Nothing really helps much, does it?"

Impulsively, Marti hugged Mom, holding tightly, needing the strength of her mother's arms around her. "I miss Barry so much," she mumbled.

"Oh, darling, of course you do," Mom said.

"I think about him all the time. Even when I'm sleeping. Over and over I have the same dream. Barry thinks he's alone in the house, but someone else is there too. It's a dark shadow that creeps up on Barry, and I'm supposed to stop the shadow, but I can't. And I try to scream, but I can't. And I wake up crying because I wonder if there was something I could have done to help Barry."

"Marti, you mustn't confuse your dreams with the truth," Mom said. "There's nothing you—" There was an impatient toot of a horn in the driveway, and Mom made a quick grab for her briefcase. "We'll try to find time to talk tonight," she said. "Your father's impatient. He's got an early meeting." She planted a kiss that slid off Marti's right ear, and added as she whirled toward the door, "Marti, you *must* go to school. It's the only way to handle it."

"I will," Marti promised. She couldn't think of a good reason not to.

But later, when the entire student body was called to the cafetorium for an assembly, she was sorry for that promise. Mr. Billingsly, the balding, rotund principal of Farrington Park High School, conducted a short memorial for Barry, which turned out to be more of an embarrassed apology that one of Farrington Park's finest, most promising students had been so misguided as to take his own life. Marti dug her fingernails into the palms of her hands, concentrating on the pain, refusing to listen to what Mr. Billingsly was saying.

She was thankful when he bowed his head and called for one minute of silence. All she wanted was to get out of this place. She was tired and dizzy, and as she stared at the little specks in the asphalt tile floor, they began to quiver and wiggle. Marti squirmed on the bench, and Kim, who was squeezed tightly next to her, touched her arm. "Hang on," Kim whispered. "There's not much more he can say."

But Kim was wrong. Mr. Billingsley suddenly raised his head with a look of relief, as though he'd been counting the seconds, and announced, "Many of you have heard of Dr. Clement Granberry, a nationally known psychologist who has written a number of best-selling self-help books. Dr. Granberry has become concerned with the rising number of teenage suicides across the United States and is gathering information for a book exploring the problem. He contacted me after learning through the news media about Barry Logan's suicide and graciously asked to speak to—"

Marti stumbled to her feet, shouting, "No! It's not true! It's a lie!"

Mr. Billingsly's mouth, pink and fleshy, hung limply open as he and Marti goggled at each other over a

23

waving sea of hundreds of pairs of wide-open, shocked eyes. Marti clapped her hands to the sides of her head and screamed, "Barry didn't kill himself! He didn't! Barry was murdered!"

CHAPTER • 3

Marti felt herself being led from the room, someone's arm around her shoulders, and she didn't resist. She recognized the voice of her chemistry teacher, Miss Abrams, who murmured over and over, "You'll be all right, Marti. You'll be all right."

I am all right. It's everybody else who's wrong. Marti realized she had spoken the words only in her mind, but it didn't matter. Miss Abrams would be like everyone else. She wouldn't believe her, either.

A door opened and then another, and the school nurse was gently pushing her down onto a cot. "Just lie down here for a while, Marti," the nurse said in a cheery voice. "Your color's good, but we'll take your temperature and blood pressure in a few minutes and just let you rest until you feel better."

Marti did as she was told, lying back and closing her

eyes. She let out a long sigh. She was so terribly tired. The two women went into the next room, but Marti could hear their whispers: "They were close friends. It scares me to death. What if she—?"

"It's probably just stress."

"I hope so. I keep thinking about that copycat theory. I mean, so many, many kids. Someone commits suicide, and others follow. It's horrifying. I can't believe they really understand what they're doing."

"All I can do is make sure Marti doesn't need medical care. We'll have her talk to her senior counselor. As a matter of fact, Betty will probably be in here looking for Marti as soon as the assembly's over. Betty's going to be working with that Granberry fellow on his book. Did she tell you?"

"The book on suicides? Nobody's told me anything. You mean Betty's going to help write that book?"

"Just research stuff. That kind of thing. She's going to tie it into the project she's doing for her doctorate."

"Speaking of which—guess who else is going for the degree?"

The topic of their conversation shifted, and Marti tuned them out. She was furious with herself. She wanted people to listen, to take seriously what she had to tell them, and she had blown it when she had acted like that in assembly. Now she was back to zero. *But I won't give up,* she promised herself.

"Marti."

Marti opened her eyes to see Mrs. Allen, the school nurse, standing over her. "Open your mouth, dear. We're going to take your temperature."

In a short time the digital thermometer registered, and Mrs. Allen said, "Normal. Just what I thought."

Next the blood-pressure cuff was snugly wrapped on

Marti's upper right arm. Mrs. Allen seemed to be pleased with the reading.

"So here she is." A voice spoke from the doorway.

Marti looked up to see Elizabeth Dillard, the senior-class counselor. Marti had met with Miss Dillard briefly to go over her senior schedule and to get information about college applications, but she really didn't know the woman. Miss Dillard was shaped something like a pear. Her head was small, and with her hair pulled back tightly, it looked even smaller. Her shoulders were narrow, her chest almost flat, but her hips and thighs spread out magnificently. Mr. Billingsly had made the mistake in assembly last year of mentioning that, in regard to student problems, Miss Dillard had a very broad understanding. After the initial snickers had subsided, his words became an "in" joke for the entire senior class, and Marti couldn't look at the woman without mentally attaching the label. Miss Dillard's smile was pleasant, but Marti wondered how she really felt about the joke.

"Marti checks out physically," Mrs. Allen said to Miss Dillard. "I'm guessing the stress just got to be a little too much for her."

With one finger, Miss Dillard pushed her glasses back up her nose to peer at Marti. "Would you like to come into my office and talk with me?" she asked.

"Yes," Marti said. She stood up a little too quickly, swaying for just an instant as she fought to regain her equilibrium. She saw Miss Dillard glance at her sharply before she led the way to her office. Marti followed close behind her.

Miss Dillard seated herself behind her desk, waved toward the only other chair in the room, and leaned forward intently as Marti sat down. "Let's be open and

27

straightforward with each other," she said. "If you're on something, tell me."

"I don't do drugs," Marti said. "I'm not stupid."

Again the inquisitive, searching look before Miss Dillard asked, "Not even once in a while? Not even with your friend, Barry Logan?"

Marti fought the hot anger that welled up, flushing her cheeks and forehead. It was important to stay calm. "No. Barry didn't use drugs, either."

Miss Dillard picked up a pencil and flipped it back and forth between two fingers. "Studies have shown," she said, "that in many cases, when a good and popular student takes his life, abuse of drugs was involved."

"We're not talking about 'studies.' We're talking about Barry, and you can take my word for it. I knew Barry, and I would have known it if he'd ever done drugs."

"I'm sorry, Marti," Miss Dillard said, and she sighed. "Unfortunately, it's a question that can't be dismissed lightly."

Marti shook her head. "The question doesn't even matter," she answered. "I know I sounded off in assembly when I shouldn't have, but what I said is true. Barry didn't commit suicide."

Miss Dillard paused as though she were trying to find the right words before she answered. "Marti, I know this is terribly hard for you, and I sympathize. Maybe it would help you to understand that there are various stages toward the acceptance of death of a loved one. The first are anger and denial."

Marti slid to the edge of her chair and leaned her forearms on Miss Dillard's desk. "Please listen to me," she begged. "Someone has to listen."

"I'm listening. That's what I'm here for."

"Okay, then." Marti took a long breath and said, "Forget all the rules and labels in your psychology books. I'm talking about a person, not a case. I know that Barry didn't kill himself. I'm trying to do something to prove it."

"Surely the police and coroner's office would be better able to know how—"

Marti jumped to her feet. "But they don't know! They didn't even know he was left-handed." She shook her head. "That doesn't matter right now. The important thing is that Barry had no reason to kill himself. Can't you understand?"

A film came over Miss Dillard's eyes, and the corners of her mouth softened. "My favorite uncle killed himself," she said quietly. "I was younger than you—eleven —and for a long time I couldn't make myself believe it. I'd invent stories in which he was off on a trip to some marvelous country, and he'd come home and walk toward me with his arms held out." She stopped speaking for a few moments, and Marti could see the muscles in her throat work as she gulped, trying to regain control over her emotions.

"I'm sorry," Marti murmured.

When Miss Dillard spoke, her voice was back to normal. "As you see, the memories still are painful. However, the point I'm trying to make is that I had to face the truth, and you must too."

Marti shook her head. "People who kill themselves are depressed. They can't take it anymore. They don't have any hope left. Isn't that right?" Without waiting for an answer she continued. "Barry didn't have any of those reasons. He'd just gotten his early acceptance letter from Texas A & M, and he was really happy about it. He asked me last week if I wanted to go in fifty-fifty with him and give a Halloween party, and he talked about a camp job he was going to try to get next summer. He wasn't making all those plans and at the same time thinking about committing suicide."

As Miss Dillard listened she poked at her chin with the eraser end of a pencil. Finally she said, "You knew Barry well?"

"Very well. We lived next door to each other. We'd been good friends ever since our families moved here."

"Do you know of other suicides in his family?"

"I'm sure there weren't any, or someone would have said so. Barry never talked about any."

"Hmm. No depression, no drugs, no family history of suicidal behavior." Miss Dillard put down her pencil and waved toward the empty chair. "Sit down, Marti. Please. What you've told me is very interesting."

"Then help me," Marti said. She slowly lowered herself to the edge of the chair and waited. Maybe this was it. Maybe Miss Dillard would understand.

Miss Dillard bent over her desk, making some notations with her pencil on a lined pad of paper. When she looked up at Marti she said, "Maybe there *is* something I can do to help you. Let me give you a little background first. I've been doing some intensive research on teen suicides and plan to write my doctoral dissertation on the subject. I became interested in this social problem when two of our students committed suicide last year. Did you know them?"

"Yes," Marti said.

"Very well. You may not know this, Marti, but they fit into a pattern that researchers have noted. The students exhibited depressive symptoms, apparently due to the ending of their physical relationship; they showed a change in sleep or appetite, along with a certain amount of aggressive and impulsive behavior; and it was established that they both had a history of mild drug abuse." She sighed again. "It doesn't take much," she added, and slid her glasses back into place on the bridge of her nose.

Marti shivered. "You make it sound so technical. We're talking about Robin and Al," she said. "They were people."

"Oh, Marti," Miss Dillard said, "I don't mean to sound like a textbook. Believe me, when they died it was such a shock and hurt so much—" She took a deep breath and said, more calmly, "Maybe talking about suicide in technical terms is a way of stepping back, of getting away from the pain."

"I-I think I know what you mean."

"What you've been telling me about Barry leads me to believe that he may not have exhibited some of the warning signs. Was he friends with either of the students?"

"Yes. He was on the tennis team with Al, but—"

Miss Dillard propped her elbows on her desk and rested her chin on her fists. "Have you heard of the term *copycat suicide*?"

Marti gasped and slid to the edge of her chair. "If you mean Barry, he didn't—" Marti stopped. "You don't believe me."

Miss Dillard leaned forward, her hands gripped together so tightly that her knuckles were white. "Listen to me, Marti. Don't go. Listen. I should have gotten right to the point. After your—uh—after you were so upset, Dr. Clement Granberry asked about you. He's quite interested in talking with you."

"But I don't want to talk to him." Marti stood and walked to the door.

31

Miss Dillard struggled to her feet. "I understand. I really do. Right now you're under a great deal of stress, and it's hard for you to think clearly about what happened to your friend. But Dr. Granberry will be staying in Farrington Park for a while. Please consider meeting him and listening to what he has to say. He's making a detailed study of teen suicides, and I really believe that he can help you accept the truth of the situation."

Marti didn't try to explain that she was *never* going to meet with Dr. Granberry if she could help it. She walked from the office and into the main hall as Miss Dillard called after her, "Marti, I want to help you. Remember, I'll be right here anytime you need me."

Kim appeared at her side. "I waited for you," she said.

"You cut class?"

"It wasn't going to be much of a class. Just a review on world events. I don't think the countries of the world know what they're doing themselves, so how should anyone expect me to?"

Marti couldn't help smiling. She headed toward her locker, Kim at her side.

"So how'd it go with the broad understanding?" Kim asked.

"She tried to help me understand that my faith in Barry is all wrong."

Kim looked down as her face flushed red. "Look, Marti, I—"

"It's okay," Marti said. "I'm just letting you know that you aren't the only one who doesn't believe me."

Kim took a deep breath, and Marti could almost see her change gears. "The bell's going to ring for lunch pretty soon," Kim said. "Let's get to the cafeteria before the mob arrives."

Marti shook her head. "I'm not hungry."

"You have to eat something," Kim said, "whether you want to or not."

Marti didn't feel like arguing. She let Kim take charge and even ate what Kim ordered for her. Later she thought it might have been vegetable soup. It didn't matter.

The day went badly. Marti couldn't concentrate. In English literature she had to stammer, "I'm sorry. I didn't hear what you said," to Mr. Thompson.

Mr. Thompson—who'd been teaching for as long as anyone could remember, and who had good-naturedly started the semester by explaining that the reason for his total baldness was that all the activity went on *inside* his head and not on the outside—simply nodded patiently before tossing the question at someone else.

Marti felt someone staring and glanced over to see Emmet Miller's gaze fixed upon her. Same olive-green eyes as his brother Thad's, but in a thinner, narrower face. Emmet immediately dropped his glance to his book and hunched over it.

"How many looked up the quotes I gave you last week?"

Most of the hands went up, so Mr. Thompson said, "Okay. Then you know they're from Coleridge's 'Kubla Khan.' Now, if we look for sensory perception in 'Kubla Khan' . . ." He went on, and Marti tried to follow his explanation.

She began to wonder about Emmet. Most of the people in this class had attended Barry's funeral, but not Emmet. As Thad Miller's little brother, just one year younger, he'd spent years tagging after Thad, Barry, Charlie, and Tony, even though they'd usually chased him away. Sometimes she'd felt sorry for Emmet, who

looked so eager to belong, so lonely without his brother.
Once, when the Cuatros had been in Barry's backyard
and had loudly jeered at Emmet and told him to get
lost, she'd climbed up in the elm tree, where they could
see her, and shouted at them that they were pigs.

"Why are you so mean to Emmet?" she'd yelled, but
they'd laughed and yelled insults back at her. Even
Emmet—who had only reached the gate—had furi-
ously screeched at Marti to mind her own business.

She had climbed down from the tree, skinning her
right knee and grumbling that boys could be horrible to
each other. Later Barry had brought over a fistful of his
mother's home-made chocolate-chip cookies, and she'd
easily forgiven him. She really didn't blame them for
not wanting Emmet around. She wouldn't have liked it,
either.

After Thad had left Farrington Park, Marti hadn't
seen much of Emmet. There was nothing unusual
about that. Emmet had his own friends in his own class.
He was a quiet person and usually kept to himself, but it
was odd that he hadn't gone to Barry's funeral. He
could have given Barry that much.

Marti was grateful when the final bell rang and she
could head for home. She walked briskly, swallowed by
the flow of others who poured from the building.

"Marti, wait!" Kim squeezed and elbowed until she
was beside her. "I'll walk you home."

"Your house is in the opposite direction."

"I need the walk. I'm trying to lose weight."

Marti shook her head. "I don't need a shadow. I'm not
going to do anything dumb."

"I know you won't." Kim dropped her books and
stooped to pick them up again. "We're good friends,
Marti," she said. "I think you'd like to have someone

34

with you, and I want it to be me." She shifted her weight to her right foot and her books, off-balance, tumbled to the ground again.

This time Marti helped Kim pick them up and tucked them firmly into her arms. "I don't need help as much as you do," she said.

A girl rushed past them, calling, "You're going to be late, Kim. Better hurry up."

Kim did a bad job of trying to look innocently surprised, and Marti couldn't help smiling. "Remember what day this is? You're supposed to meet with the Yearbook committee."

"I know, but—"

"I'm tired, Kim," Marti said, "and I'd like to sleep for a while before Mom and Dad get home. Honest. I didn't sleep much last night, and I really need to now. Don't worry about me. Go to your meeting."

Kim studied her for a moment. "I'm not going to worry about you, Marti," she said. "But if you want me to come over later, just call. Okay?"

"Okay," Marti answered. She turned and walked down the now deserted sidewalk, feeling Kim's eyes on her back until she turned the corner.

She was the only one on the wide street, which wound in a circular fashion to meet other streets, which formed their own semicircles. Clusters of pines, purple-leaved flowering plum, and crepe myrtle, planted along the median strip in the center of the street, were growing tall enough to provide shade, and landscaped front yards bloomed with bright touches of purslane and periwinkle, flowers strong enough to last through the summer's heat. For once, Marti didn't mind the houses with their empty glass eyes. She felt as empty as the houses. She was a hollow shell that walked through a silent, lonely void.

Marti heard the low throb of the automobile motor long before it registered on her mind that the car hadn't passed her. Its purr in the far background was a steady, unchanging hum, and she glanced over her shoulder to see a nondescript and dusty light gray sedan idling near the curb far back at the corner where she had turned. With sunlight glinting against the windshield, it was impossible to see the driver. Someone waiting for a friend, no doubt.

She walked on, going over in her mind the unhappy conversation with Miss Dillard, until she realized the sound of the automobile motor was still with her. She stopped and turned to look back. The car was near the curb, but it had moved to keep pace with her. She gripped her books tightly and tried to tell herself that the driver of that car—whoever it might be—had nothing to do with her. Deliberately, she turned and walked on, her steps a little quicker.

As Marti reached the next corner she glanced back again, this time furtively. The car was creeping up the street behind her. Now she knew for sure that she was being followed. But why?

The driver was keeping enough distance between them so that she couldn't see who was behind the wheel. Whoever it was must know that she was aware of the car. So why didn't the driver move closer? Make himself known?

Or would he, before she reached the safety of her home?

Marti stumbled over a lawn hose that was stretched across the sidewalk, dropped her chemistry book, and fumbled, trying to pick it up. Frantically she glanced back, but the car hadn't come nearer.

One more quiet street, one more curve. Mentally, she checked off the inhabitants of each of the houses she would pass. The Coopers—they had children in day-care who wouldn't be picked up until six. The Tuckers —an older couple. Mrs. Tucker had told Marti's mother they'd be traveling through Europe during September. The Martins, the Cohens—both couples working in Houston. The Logans—would Mrs. Logan be home? No. Mom had said that Mrs. Logan, on the advice of her doctor, was going to stay away from her house for a while, so Mr. Logan had taken her to visit her sister in San Antonio. If Marti shouted, no one would hear her. There was no one to help her. No one to see her. Just the row of empty houses with their blank windowpane eyes.

It hurt to breathe as she gulped short, shallow gasps of air. Marti walked quickly, running at times, constantly aware of the never-changing sound of the car that kept pace behind her like a hovering shadow. She twisted often to look over her shoulder. Was it coming closer?

When she reached the Logans' front lawn she broke into a sprint. Crying and whimpering with fear, she scrambled up the front steps of her house, grabbed for her front-door key, and dropped it.

The sound of the car's engine grew louder. She heard the car slowly getting nearer, creeping toward her like a cat ready to pounce on a mouse. With numb, wooden fingers she managed to retrieve the key, poke it into the lock, and turn it. She flung the door open, jerked out the key, slammed the door, and locked it just as the car pulled up in front of her house.

Terrified, Marti leaned against the door, gasping for breath as her heart thudded against her ribs. Who was it who had followed her? Who was out there?

Clinging to the door, she twisted to peer through the narrow strip of leaded glass panes that decorated the entryway. Vision through the glass was distorted, but Marti could see that the car had left. The street in front of her house was empty.

The glass was chill against Marti's damp forehead. The cold made it easier to think, as though it drew to itself little sharp-edged thoughts that popped from a sluggish mind as dense as thickening gelatin. Why should she be afraid of the driver of that car? There were a number of perfectly sensible reasons why the car should have been there. The driver could have been someone who was lost and trying to find an address. Maybe it was a real-estate agent, looking over the neighborhood. Someone playing a prank.

Or someone who wanted to follow her home.

When the telephone rang, jangling into the silence, Marti jumped and let out a screech, dropping her books with a crash onto the tile floor of the entry hall. Scrambling, stumbling, she ran to the den and picked up the receiver.

"Hello!" she shouted.

"Marti?" a woman's voice inquired.

"This is Marti."

"This is Karen Prescott."

"I—I didn't think I'd ever hear from you."

"Why not? I said I'd give some thought to what you told me."

"That sounded like a turn-off."

"I meant what I said."

There was a pause before Marti murmured, "I'm sorry. I keep saying the wrong things."

"It's a common problem." For a moment there was a touch of laughter, of camaraderie, in Karen's voice, and Marti smiled in answer.

Karen continued. "I'd like to come over to your house and talk to you, Marti. I've done a little preliminary investigating, and some information I've come across has brought up a question."

Marti gripped the telephone receiver tightly and tried not to shout into it. "What kind of a question? What do you mean?"

"Calm down," Karen said. "It's not much to go on. It's just something in the medical examiner's report that makes me wonder."

"What are you talking about?"

"About the cause of Barry Logan's death. There seems to be a slight possibility," Karen said, "that you could be right."

CHAPTER · 4

Karen was wearing her uniform, a holstered gun at her hip. Marti had to pull her eyes away from the gun. It set Karen apart; it gave her such authority that Marti suddenly became shy.

"W-would you like something to drink?" she stammered, trying to think of the right thing to say as she led Karen into the den. "We've got some diet colas."

"No, thanks," Karen answered. "I'd rather get right to business." She sat on the nearest armchair.

Marti perched on the chair opposite and wished Karen didn't look so young. Karen was a couple of inches shorter than Marti and not as slender, and with that short-cropped curly hair and freckled nose she could have passed for a high-school student. But there was something positive about the way Karen moved and sat and spoke. As their eyes met, Marti recognized the strength and directness of a woman who was used to being in charge, and she knew that she was being studied in turn. She began to relax. Maybe Karen *would* be able to help.

Marti spoke first. "You said you believe me now about Barry."

"I said you could be right."

"It's the same thing."

Karen shook her head. "No, it isn't. There's a big *if* in what I said."

Disappointed, Marti blurted, "If you don't believe me, then why are you here?"

For a moment Karen just stared at her, then quietly asked, "Do you know anything about the way police conduct an investigation?"

"I guess not." Marti was suddenly embarrassed.

"It's a matter of dealing in facts. Collecting them. Adding them up. That's what I'm doing. That's what you asked me to do. Right?"

"Yes."

"Then let's get with it."

Marti nodded, wishing she could rub away the heat that had spread through her face. "I'm sorry," she mumbled. She saw Karen's expression soften.

"It's okay," Karen said.

Marti smiled ruefully. "I keep apologizing. I don't mean to be rude. I guess I don't stop and think. If we could only prove that Barry—" She took a long, deep breath and added, "There's only one part of me that seems to exist anymore. I don't expect you to know what I mean."

"But I do," Karen answered.

She spoke with such conviction that Marti murmured, "Why?"

"When I was twelve," Karen said, "my best friend was on her way to my house on her bike when she was killed by a hit-and-run driver. I became obsessed with trying to find the person. I studied cars in parking lots, looking for dents in the bumper. I stared at faces on the street, hoping—I guess—that there would be some sign to label the killer. I wanted the person to be caught, and it was all I could think about."

She stopped, and Marti asked, "Did you find the driver?"

"No," Karen said, "and neither did the police. Then when you came into the station and told me your story, in a way it was like seeing myself twelve years ago."

Aching, Marti wanted to reach out to Karen, but instead she simply mumbled, "Thanks for telling me."

"I'd planned to," Karen said. "I thought it might help if you knew." She continued to look at Marti for a brief moment, then briskly brushed a strand of hair from her forehead, once more becoming businesslike. "Okay— now for the information I have for you. Today was my day off, so I went to the coroner's office in Houston and read the autopsy report."

"An autopsy? On Barry?" Marti's right hand automatically went to her throat, and she felt a little sick. "Isn't that when they—? Why'd they have to do that to Barry?"

"It's mandatory in any case of unnatural death."

As Marti shuddered, Karen leaned forward and placed a hand on her arm. "This is going to be rough on you. I'd make it easier if I could, but I can't. I'm sorry."

Marti sat up a little straighter. "As you said, this is what I asked you to do. Go on."

Karen gave a brisk nod. "All right. First of all, they found no trace of drugs."

"Barry didn't do drugs. Why would they even look for drugs?"

"Because many people who end their lives are under the influence of drugs or alcohol. Normally, they probably could handle their depression, but the drugs cloud their thinking and can send them over the edge."

Marti gripped the arms of her chair. "Could that be why Robin . . . why Al—?"

"Judging from information in their files, I'd say drugs may have been a factor," Karen said. She paused for only a moment. "I studied their autopsy reports and went over their files carefully, so before you ask the next question, I'll tell you that I don't think there's any doubt that they took their own lives. But as for Barry—"

Marti tensed.

"There was a bruise at the back of Barry's head. I won't read you the medical report, because it's long and detailed and technical. What it comes down to is that the bruise occurred while Barry was still alive, and it was severe enough to have caused a concussion. It was the only bruise on his body."

"They can tell when Barry was bruised?"

"Yes. Now, let me ask you a question. Do you know if Barry had a fall? If he'd been in a fight? Was there any way you know of that he could have received that bruise on his head shortly before his death?"

"No." Marti suddenly gasped. "Wait a minute! Are you thinking that he might have had a fight with the person who killed him? Is that it?"

"There were no signs of a fight. In fact, there were no signs of forced entry, no evidence that anyone other than Barry had been in the house."

Marti snapped up as though her spine were a rubber band and paced back and forth from her chair to the fireplace. Like a recurring fog, her dream slid through her mind. The shadow creeping up on Barry. The shadow she couldn't stop. She twined her fingers together tightly to keep them from trembling. "I know what it might mean," Marti said. "Barry let someone he knew into the house, and that person knocked Barry unconscious by hitting him on the back of the head, then staged the suicide scene."

"Take it easy. We're talking about possibilities only."

Marti stood in front of Karen, her hands still clenched. "What does the coroner think?"

"The medical examiner in the coroner's office who did the autopsy wrote up Barry's death as a suicide."

"But the bruise—"

"I talked to the man, but he felt the bruise was irrelevant, and he had no intention of changing his report. There were powder burns on Barry's head near the bullet's point of entry; his fingerprints were on the gun; and the paraffin test showed nitrates on his right hand, which proved he was holding the gun when it was fired."

"His *right* hand," Marti repeated.

"I remembered. You told me Barry was left-handed."

"Can't we just tell everybody what we found out? Can't the police start looking for Barry's murderer?"

"No," Karen said. "The district attorney's office can't make a case without a wrongful death report from the coroner, which means our small police department can't expend the time or money it takes to work on the case."

"That's not right. It's not fair. Just because one person decides that—" Marti began to pace again.

Karen stood and intercepted Marti, holding her by the shoulders. "Calm down," she said. "I didn't come

here to tell you to forget it. I came to find out as much as
I could from you. We may uncover something that
could give us a lead."

"You're going to keep investigating?"

"As much as I can. As you could see when you visited
the station, we're not that busy in Farrington Park. I
have a routine patrol to drive and a certain number of
calls to follow through on. Most of them involve aban-
doned vehicles or suspicious persons or house doors left
open—mostly situations that turn out to be nothing to
worry about. Occasionally there's a traffic accident, a
break-in, maybe a shoplifter caught in the mall. It's a
necessary job, but on the whole not a terribly demand-
ing one."

"So now this investigation will be part of your job?"

Karen shook her head. "I was just giving you some
background, so you'd understand. My point is that this
case was assigned to Sergeant Bill Nieman, not to me,
and since the case has been closed, there'd be no way I
could get official approval for any full-scale investigation. Because there are some unanswered questions
here, I've decided to try to take some time on my own
to see what turns up."

"If you do this in your spare time, won't your family
object?"

Karen shook her head. "I have no family in Houston.
I live alone." Her words were matter-of-fact, but for
just an instant Marti saw a shadow in Karen's eyes and
recognized it as the same loneliness she felt.

"Want that diet Coke now?" Marti asked.

Karen smiled. "I guess I do."

As they walked out to the kitchen Marti said, "It
makes it a little easier, knowing that you're on my side."

"I investigate," Karen said. "I don't take sides." But she smiled again.

They sat at the kitchen table, where they could look through the sliding glass-doors to the expanse of neatly clipped saint augustine grass, which was bordered with sprawling azalea, Indian hawthorn, and hibiscus shrubs, all past the blooming season. A weathered, faded pink geranium drooped in its pot near the edge of the patio, and heat waves shimmered from the top of the shining metal gas grill.

Karen raised her can of cola. "Here's to air-conditioning," she said.

Marti rested her elbows on the table and slid the icy, beaded can against her cheek. "Right about now Barry and I would be going swimming. He has a pool in his backyard, you know. We used to see who could swim more laps."

"Don't do this to yourself," Karen said. "I'm going to need you to think clearly, not emotionally."

Marti's voice came out like a sob. "How do you get past the emotion?"

"I don't know. But you're going to have to try."

Marti placed her can of cola on the table and wiped her hands on her jeans. "Is it hard to be a cop? Is it hard to be tough?"

For an instant Karen looked hurt and even younger. She shrugged. "I don't think of myself as tough. I just try to do my job," she said.

"Well, I didn't exactly mean—"

"Police have to deal with a lot of hurting, frightened people," Karen said. "It takes just an instant for someone to become a victim, for lives to be destroyed. Often, when I was working a beat in Houston, I'd see things that would tear me up inside. But I'd save the tears until I was alone. When my partner and I had work to do, the work had to come first. There wasn't a choice."

"Tell me about your partner," Marti said. "Was she young, like you?"

"*He.* He *is* young, and he's a good cop."

"A good friend?"

Karen's cheeks grew pink, and she quickly said, "We're getting sidetracked, and we've got work to do." She pulled a small notepad and a pen from her shirt pocket. "If you're ready, let's get to the questions. At this time we'll work under the assumption—I repeat, *assumption*— that someone did kill Barry. If this were the case, then, judging by the evidence, most likely it would have been someone he knew. You're probably better acquainted with the people Barry knew than anyone else. So tell me, who were Barry's enemies?"

Marti put her hands to her forehead and squeezed her eyes shut, trying to think of everyone Barry knew. Finally, she gave a long sigh and collapsed against the straight back of the kitchen chair. "Barry didn't have enemies. Everybody liked Barry."

"You said he was on a tennis team. Any angry rivalries? Someone who thought Barry had cheated him?"

"No. Everybody knew that Barry wouldn't cheat anyone. He was a good player, and fair. And he wasn't that competitive. He was more likely to laugh it off if he lost." Marti scowled. "Wouldn't that be kind of weird? To have someone who lost a tennis match want to kill the winner?"

"We have to try every angle," Karen answered. "Something you remember may give us a clue. Now, how about the people where Barry worked part-time? Did he ever tell you about a conflict with any of them? Was there ever an argument? Any hard feelings?"

The questions went on and on until Marti, exhausted, folded her arms on the table and rested her head on them. "No!" she said. "Barry wasn't the kind of guy to get into trouble. You can ask anybody." She raised her head and blinked at Karen.

The clock in the hall chimed into the silence while Karen scribbled something in her notebook. "Give me some names," Karen said.

"Okay. There's the tennis coach and the senior counselor—" Marti went down a list, ticking names of responsible adults on her fingers and adding Charlie and Tony as Barry's closest friends.

"That should do it for now," Karen finally said.

Marti got up and stretched, rubbing the back of her neck. "I've got to make dinner. Mom and Dad come home hungry. Would you like to stay and have dinner with us?"

Karen stood too, and tucked her notebook and pen back into her pocket. "No, thanks."

"We didn't get very far, did we?"

"It's a start." Karen smiled and handed Marti a business card. "I wrote my home phone number on the back. It's in Houston, so you'll have to dial *1* first. If you think of something else, if you have any questions, you can reach me at the Farrington Park station or at home."

"Thanks for all you're doing," Marti said. She walked with Karen to the front door. "If you can just find out the truth about what happened to Barry—"

Her voice trailed off, but Karen reached out to pat her shoulder briskly. "We'll do our best to get the answers," she said. "That's all I can promise."

"That's enough. Will you call to let me know if you find out anything that helps?"

49

"Of course. I'll keep in touch."

Marti watched Karen walk to her car before she closed and locked the door. Remembering the car that had frightened her, she briefly wondered if she should have told Karen about it; but all she could picture was a hysterical girl whimpering and racing and stumbling down the street for no real reason. No one had accosted her or threatened her. Marti sighed. Karen would probably put it down to an overactive imagination, and at the moment, Marti was inclined to agree.

Marti returned to the kitchen and pulled a package of chicken breasts from the meat drawer of the refrigerator. Tossing onto the counter some margarine, lemon juice, and an onion, she began to assemble the ingredients she'd need for dinner. She'd have to hurry if she wanted everything ready by the time her parents got home.

As she usually did, in order to break the lonely silence of the house, Marti flipped on the small television set on the side counter. She often watched reruns on Channel 26 or 39, but the channel selector was set to one of the network affiliates that was televising an early local news program. Holding a tin of powdered ginger, a box of rice, and a can of peas, Marti stopped still and stared at the familiar face on the screen. It was Dr. Jerome Emery, their family friend, the pastor of their church.

"It's time that someone began a crusade," Dr. Emery was saying, his voice vibrating with intensity, "against the evil that is being sold to our children under the guise of music. Three fine young people in our neighborhood, good students from moral homes, all of them so hypnotized by the hopelessness, by the death wish— oh, I've listened to the lyrics!—of this devil-worshipping rock group called Flesh, that they took their own lives."

"No!" Marti shouted at the face of a man so kind and caring that the pain of his feelings glittered in his eyes. "You don't understand!"

Dr. Emery, seemingly unaware of the camera that was trained on him, ran his fingers through his thick shock of white hair, giving himself the appearance of someone who had just climbed out of bed. Marti had seen him do this when he was intent on what he was saying, and she had also seen the fond, exasperated glances from his wife. "I keep telling him," Mrs. Emery had once murmured, "but it doesn't do any good. When Jerome puts his heart and mind and energies into something, he cares too much to worry about his appearance."

"I plan to go to the people, to the churches, to the media, for help," Dr. Emery continued, in answer to a question from the newscaster. "I plan to devote every minute of my spare time to reaching good people across this country and making them aware of the dangerous and deadly spell cast over our young people by this evil music. And I dedicate this work to someone who was a member of my own congregation: the fine young man who was so influenced by this rock group that he took his own life—Barry Logan. Our memories of Barry will be my strength, my moving force, the impetus that will help me reach my goal."

Marti groaned and rested her head on the counter.

Next to her ear the telephone jangled, and she started so violently that she knocked the onion and box of rice to the floor. She grabbed the receiver and shouted, "Hello!" over the sound of the television program.

There was silence for a moment, until a voice so soft

she could barely hear it mumbled, "Good. You've been listening to the right channel."

"Who is this?" Marti demanded as she jabbed the Off button of the television set.

The caller didn't speak again, but Marti was aware of steady breathing, of someone listening.

"Who are you?" she screamed into the phone. "What do you want?"

Her only answer was a soft click as the line went dead.

CHAPTER · 5

Marti slammed down the receiver and turned her energies to the chicken, viciously poking and stabbing the pieces that were browning in the melted butter, as though they'd been responsible for the telephone call. She added the lemon juice and seasonings, turned the cook-top dial to Simmer, and slapped a lid on the pan.

Marti slumped against the counter and tried to think. Who had made that telephone call? Who wanted to make sure she heard what Dr. Emery had to say? For that matter, who didn't? Karen was the only one who came close to agreeing that Barry's death was murder, and even Karen called her probe into the facts concerning Barry's death only an investigation. Could the person who telephoned be someone cruel who wanted to taunt her? Or could it have been a friend who just wanted Marti to face the facts as everyone else saw them?

She glanced at the clock and quickly reached for the rice. She'd have to hurry. There was no time now to try to puzzle out the telephone call. Carefully, she poured water into the glass measuring-cup, holding it up and squinting to see if the water met the red line. Tomorrow, Marti reassured herself, as soon as the church offices were open, she'd make an appointment to see Dr. Emery. She had to stop him from using Barry as a symbol for his campaign.

Marti heard the electronic garage door begin to whir its way up and knew that her parents had arrived home. She stirred the rice, deciding to allow it another few minutes, and took the lid from the chicken. Expectantly, she turned toward the door that opened onto the short walkway to the garage.

When the door didn't open, she hurried to it and threw it wide, blinking to see the garage door down again and no sign of her parents.

Making sure the door wouldn't lock behind her, Marti ran across the walkway and turned the knob on the side door to the garage. The car was inside, but empty. Puzzled, Marti scowled. Where were Mom and Dad?

"Marti?" her mother called from the kitchen, and Marti whirled and ran back inside the house.

"Where were you?" the two of them asked each other at the same time.

"We picked up the Logans' mail and put it inside their house on the hall table," Marti's mother said. She shivered. "It's a good thing that Alice and Paul went away for a while. The house has such a—a *feeling.*"

As her mother tucked away the Logans' front-door key on the shelf with the good china, Marti asked, "Where's Dad?"

"Putting on his old clothes. He's going to mow the Logans' lawn as well as ours as soon as it's not quite so hot." She gave a little smile. "It's the least we can do to help."

Marti's tall, balding, and slightly stoop-shouldered father strolled into the kitchen, chin down, buttoning the last couple of buttons on a faded plaid shirt. He sniffed the air. "Something smells good," he said, and smiled.

It was the same thing he said every night, unless they had plans to go out to dinner. Marti patiently smiled back.

He glanced quickly at his wife. "Have you talked to Marti yet?"

Mom rolled her eyes up to stare with exasperation at the ceiling before she answered, "*After* dinner, Josh. Later this evening when we're more relaxed. Remember? I thought I made it clear."

"Okay, okay," Marti's father said. "I remember now, but I've got a lot on my mind. That factory case—I'll begin taking depositions tomorrow."

"So soon? I thought—"

"What are you supposed to talk to me about?" Marti blurted out.

"You *see*?" her mother said to her father. She turned to Marti and her voice became gentle again. "Miss Dillard called me, dear. She was concerned about your outburst in assembly." She raised her hands, palms out, in a conciliatory gesture and quickly added, "She didn't criticize you, Marti. She was all sympathy, believe me. She just suggested—well, we can talk about that this evening."

55

Marti slapped the lids back on the pans and leaned against the counter, her arms folded tightly across her chest, pressing against the fear and hurt that churned inside her. "No. Please tell me now. What did she suggest? I have to know now."

"It wasn't any big deal," Marti's father said. "She thought you ought to go for counseling."

"Go where for this counseling?"

"To her, for starters."

Marti groaned. "Maybe I'll get to be part of chapter seven."

"What do you mean by that?" Her mother looked puzzled.

"Did Miss Dillard tell you that she's going to help some psychologist named Strawberry or Cranberry— something like that—research a book about teen suicides, and that she's going to write a dissertation about suicides to get her degree?"

"I think you're misjudging her, Marti," Mom said. "She was quite concerned. She was worried about you."

"If you approach Miss Dillard's help with an open mind," Dad told her, "you may discover that she's more knowledgeable and therefore more highly qualified to counsel you than anyone else."

Marti's mother stepped forward and wrapped her arms around Marti. "Oh, sweetheart," she murmured, "we want you to get whatever help you need."

Marti could feel Mom's cheek warm against her own and held her mother tightly.

"We know it's so awful for you," her mother said, "and we feel so helpless."

Marti gave a long sigh. "Mom, maybe counseling would be the right thing, but not just yet. Not now. Miss

Dillard's okay, but right now we don't see things the same way."

"We're just asking you to think about it, Marti," her mother told her.

Marti felt her father clumsily patting her shoulder, and she reached for his hand. His fingers twisted around hers, and Marti felt the same sense of comfort she always did, ever since she was a little girl and knew she'd be safe as long as her parents were beside her.

"You'll have to understand that I'm not wrong about Barry," she said. "He didn't kill himself."

She felt her mother tense, and her father's fingers stiffened. Marti closed her eyes and leaned against her mother. They'd never believe her until she'd proved herself. There was only one person who could help her, and that was Karen.

The next morning at nine-thirty, between classes, Marti slipped into the office and used the pay phone to call Dr. Emery's secretary, Margaret Anderson, and make an appointment.

"How about next Tuesday?" Mrs. Anderson asked.

"That's too late!" Marti said. "I have to see Dr. Emery right away. Today!" She realized she was practically shouting into the phone and lowered her voice, stammering, "Mrs. Anderson, it's—it's important."

"If you could give me some indication of why you need to see him—"

"It's about Barry Logan," Marti said.

Marti glanced around. One of the clerks was openly staring at her, but as their eyes met, looked quickly away and began fumbling with some papers. A few students were on Marti's side of the counter, a couple with their backs to her, three of them watching her

57

with curiosity, all of them silent and listening intently. She turned away from them and hunched over the receiver, whispering hoarsely, "Please believe me. I heard Dr. Emery last night on television. He can't do what he said about—Listen, please! I know Dr. Emery will want to hear what I have to tell him."

"One moment," Mrs. Anderson answered. It was obvious that she had covered the receiver with her hand, but Marti could hear the hum of voices in the church office, one high-pitched, one lower. The hand was taken away. "Could you make it about three-thirty?"

"Yes," Marti said. "Right after school. Thank you. I'll be there." She hung up the telephone and left the office, hurrying past the eavesdroppers, who had suddenly become very busy.

At lunchtime she told Kim what she was going to do. Kim immediately said, "That's what I heard."

"You heard?"

Kim shrugged. "You know the school grapevine. Faster than satellite news on TV. Anyhow, I'll go with you to see Dr. Emery."

Marti shook her head. "No," she said. "Your face always shows exactly what you're thinking. Since you don't believe me about Barry, Dr. Emery will pick up on it."

"Then, I'll wait for you outside."

"No, thanks," Marti said. "You've got other things to do."

Tears welling at the corners of her eyes, Kim said, "I want to help you. That's what being a best friend is all about. Somebody should be with you when—" She stopped.

"You think that Dr. Emery won't listen to me either," Marti said.

"I don't know. I . . . oh, Marti, do you have to do this?"

"Yes," Marti said. "For Barry. I really have to."

Kim rubbed at the outer corners of her eyes with the knuckle of one finger. "Come over to my house afterward. Why don't you call your parents and ask if you can stay for dinner?"

"Maybe," Marti answered. Relenting as she saw the hurt expression on Kim's face, she tried to smile and said, "I'd like to come. I'll see how everything goes."

Marti arrived at her English lit. class a few minutes early, slipping into the chair at one end of the horseshoe arrangement Mr. Thompson had set up. Charlie immediately plopped into the seat next to her, and Tony sat down next to Charlie. Tony's glance darted around the room. Once he was assured that Mr. Thompson was busy with one of the students and no one was in earshot, he nudged Charlie, who leaned close to Marti and mumbled, "You've got to give this up, Marti. Leave Barry in peace. What you're doing is tough on all of us."

Marti stared at him, surprised. "Don't you think it's worse that Dr. Emery is going to use Barry as an example? I'd expect you and Tony to be just as upset as I am. The two of you were his best friends, part of the Cuatros."

Tony started. "Leave the Cuatros out of this," he muttered.

"What do you mean?" Marti asked.

Charlie glanced at Tony sharply, then shifted in his seat as though he couldn't find a comfortable spot. "Never mind," he said to Marti. "None of us are making much sense. Barry didn't know how it would be for the rest of us, or he wouldn't have done it."

59

"Dammit!" Marti hissed. "He didn't! Can't you believe that?"

"Even his own parents don't. They believe what the police and coroner said. And you have to, too."

"*I* have to?" Marti rebelled at the intensity in Charlie's voice. "Is that supposed to be an order? Does an *or else* go with that?"

Most of the others in the class had drifted into the room, choosing seats at random, as part of Mr. Thompson's plan for an unstructured seating arrangement. A few of them glanced toward Marti and Charlie.

"That's not what we mean," Charlie muttered, squirming down in his chair and shoving his long legs straight out. "We don't mind if you want to make a fool of yourself, as long as what you do doesn't involve Barry. All your talk about Barry being murdered makes us all look bad and makes you look stupid. We just want you to—"

"Who's this *we* you're talking about?"

"Who else? Tony and me. That's all."

"Barry's best friends. The Cuatros." Bitterness had slipped into her words, and Charlie flinched.

"Hey, look, Marti. We—"

"Marti," Mr. Thompson called, "there's a note here for you." He pushed his chair back from his desk and stood as the bell rang and the last stragglers slid into the remaining chairs in the horseshoe. He handed the note to her before he began his head count.

Marti unfolded it and read: *Please stop by my office after school. I'd like to talk to you.* It was signed *Elizabeth Dillard.*

Marti scrunched the note and shoved it into the pocket of her jeans. Not today. She had other things to take care of today. She took a few deep breaths, trying to calm down. She'd have to keep her mind on the work they'd be doing in class.

Mr. Thompson, as usual, mumbled names aloud, not expecting answers, as he checked off the attendance list. ". . . Emmet Miller . . . Debbie Field . . . Tony Lopez . . . Charlie . . . Marti . . . okay. All present and accounted for. One or two announcements before we get down to work. Beginning September 25, they'll be taking individual pictures for the yearbook. Those of you in the twelfth grade, you'll have two weeks to make appointments. Those of you in eleventh grade, your turn will come next. Now, turn to page 108. Let's get back to Coleridge; and, Emmet, we'll begin with you."

Marti snapped to attention. She had to keep her mind on what was going on in class. She couldn't repeat the excuse that she hadn't been listening. Emmet began a detailed answer to Mr. Thompson's question. He was bright, and he'd obviously done his homework on Coleridge. For a couple of reasons she felt a little sorry for Emmet. He didn't have many friends. He didn't seem to want many.

Emmet finished his answer, then glanced across at Marti, scowling as though he could read her mind. Guiltily, she quickly looked away.

"Debbie, suppose you read the next verse," Mr. Thompson said, and Marti tried to concentrate on the poem.

Finally, the last bell rang, and she quickly gathered up her books.

Charlie put a hand on her arm. "Marti—" he began, but she shrugged him away.

"You're not going to change my mind," she said, and made a dash for the door. She had an appointment to keep with Dr. Emery.

61

*   *   *

Dr. Emery's office was dim and cool and smelled of leather books and the pale, full-blown Peace roses that filled the white china bowl on his desk.

The smile lines at the corners of his blue eyes deepened as he followed Marti's glance to the roses. "Taking care of my roses is a relaxing hobby," he said. "I planted two new varieties last March. A full, deep pink and a yellow floribunda, but this old-fashioned Peace rose will always be one of my favorites."

Marti wasn't interested in the roses. She desperately groped for a way to tell Dr. Emery what she had in mind. "I—I saw you on television last night," she blurted out.

He leaned toward her, his forearms resting on his desk, his hands lightly clasped. "Then you know about the project I'm beginning," he said. "It means a great deal of work, a total commitment."

"Yes, but . . . you said that Barry . . . that he would be—"

"I said that I would dedicate my work to Barry."

"But you can't!" For a moment Marti closed her eyes. When she opened them she saw such sympathy on Dr. Emery's face that she wanted to cry out in agony.

"Marti," Dr. Emery said, "I know what good friends you and Barry were. You are suffering a great deal now. It's hard to accept the death of a loved one, even when it's a natural death. The process of acceptance is made even more difficult when someone takes his own life."

Marti shuddered and dug her fingertips into the arms of her chair. "Please listen to me," she begged. "What I have to tell you is important. Barry didn't kill himself! It's not right to call Barry a suicide victim, because he's not!"

There was a light tap on the door and it opened wide enough for Mrs. Anderson to poke her head in. "That woman from Channel 13 is on the phone."

"I can't talk to her now. I'll call her back," Dr. Emery said, and the door silently closed. He leaned back in his chair, sympathy carving furrows between his eyebrows, and asked, "Marti, don't you see that this attitude of yours is part of the early denial of Barry's death?"

Just what Miss Dillard had told her. Why couldn't they listen to what she was saying?

Marti perched on the edge of her chair. She tried to make herself breathe steadily and think calmly. She had to convince Dr. Emery that she was right and he was wrong in what he planned to do. "It *is* hard to get used to Barry's being gone," she said. "It hurts an awful lot. But I need to explain to you what I mean. Please let me explain."

"Of course," he told her. He patiently rested his chin on a steeple made by his fingers. "Go ahead, Marti. I'm listening."

Carefully, from the beginning, she told Dr. Emery what she had told Karen and what Karen had told her. When she finished, he sat quietly for a moment, thinking.

Finally, Dr. Emery said, "You mentioned that the coroner didn't seem to think the bruise was significant. I'd be inclined to agree with him. And as for the right hand versus the left hand holding the gun, does it really matter? We have no way of knowing what was in Barry's mind. It could be that the evil in that music had influenced him so greatly that he was not himself."

Marti gasped. "Barry didn't like that group, Flesh. He never listened to their music."

63

"But *Sudden Death,* the tape, was found in the Logans' VCR."

"Someone else put it there."

Dr. Emery stood and walked to the large bookcases that lined the wall of his study. He removed a notebook from the bottom shelf, opened it wide, and pulled out a few sheets of paper. He came back to the desk and handed the sheets to Marti. "The top sheet contains the lyrics for "Sudden Death," he said. "The pages under them contain lyrics for other songs performed by the disgusting group that calls itself Flesh. They're equally horrifying."

"I know." Marti didn't look at the papers on her lap.

"You're familiar with them, then?" As he spoke, he ran his hands through his thick white hair until it was a tousled mess. He was upset. Marti didn't want to upset him. She just wanted him to listen.

"Yes, Dr. Emery," she answered. "Flesh is one of the top groups. Everybody knows their tapes."

"They mock all that is good. They worship evil. In *Sudden Death* they glorify suicide."

"I know."

"Then how can you in good conscience ask me not to pursue my campaign?"

"I didn't ask you that."

"Isn't that what this appointment was for? How could I misunderstand what you've been saying?"

"I don't know." Marti leaned back and groaned. "Dr. Emery, if you want to go after Flesh, I'll support you. Their stuff is junk. Sickening junk. And chances are you're right that Flesh's music may have had something to do with Robin's and Al's suicides. At least we know both of them were playing *Sudden Death* at the time.

What I've been asking you is only that you not use Barry's name in your campaign. It's not fair of you to talk about Barry's *suicide,* when he *didn't* kill himself."

Dr. Emery was silent for a long time. Marti could hear the steady tick of a little clock on the bookcase, and the fragrance of the roses was overpowering. Finally Dr. Emery said, "You told me that you feel a commitment to Barry, but so do I. I never met the two young people who killed themselves last spring, but I knew Barry Logan well. He was a member of this congregation, a fine young man with great potential. If he had come to me—" His voice broke, but he took a deep breath and added, "In some way I failed him."

"No! You didn't," Marti interrupted.

Dr. Emery held up a hand and continued, "I can only cling to the thought that Barry would regret what he did and want to help others in any way he could. He would want to be an example to other teenagers of how the evil of that music can permeate young people's minds and actions, their very lives. After a great deal of prayer and thought, I have chosen this way for him."

"I understand how you feel, but I wish . . . oh, how I wish you could believe me!" Marti whispered.

His eyes were hurt. "Marti, don't you realize that the shock and confusion and pain you're experiencing because of Barry's death are keeping you from thinking clearly?"

"I told you what I know about Barry. I thought you would—"

But Dr. Emery got to his feet and asked, "Are your parents aware of your—your belief?"

"Yes," Marti answered.

"Are they arranging some kind of counseling for you?"

"We talked about it."

He bent to scribble a name and telephone number on a notepad, tore off the sheet, and handed it to Marti. "Let me recommend an excellent therapist," he said.

Marti took the paper, folded it, and tucked it into her pocket next to the note from Mrs. Dillard. "Please think about what I told you," she said. She felt her eyes moisten and she gulped, steadying herself with a deep breath.

Dr. Emery placed a hand on Marti's shoulder, gradually moving her toward the door. "I fully expect to meet a great deal of opposition to my work," he said. "And I know that sometimes opposition crops up in unexpected places. But this conversation has taken me by surprise. Perhaps it has served an important purpose in reminding me that the young people of today are totally unaware of the dangers of the negative, evil music that permeates their lives."

"Dr. Emery, I thought I made it clear that I don't like Flesh's music, and neither did Barry."

He opened the door and held it wide for Marti. Before he could say a word, Mrs. Anderson looked up. Her eyes sparkled with excitement. "Oh, Dr. Emery," she said. "Someone from NBC in New York called just a minute ago. I took his number. I said you'd call back."

Marti fought back the tears as she looked at Dr. Emery. "Please understand," she said. "I still want us to be friends."

His face softened and he placed his hands on her shoulders. "Of course we're friends," he said. "You're suffering a great deal of torment, Marti, and my prayers will be with you. In turn, please pray for me."

Marti didn't answer. A sob rose in her throat and she turned away, fumbling in her handbag for a tissue. The suffering a great deal of torment, Marti, and my prayers will be with you. In turn, please pray for me."

Marti didn't answer. A sob rose in her throat and she turned away, fumbling in her handbag for a tissue. The telephone rang again, and Mrs. Anderson answered it. As she placed her hand over the receiver, her voice trembled with excitement. "This time it's someone from that Monday-night TV magazine program," she said. "You can take the call in your office."

As Dr. Emery closed his office door behind him, Mrs. Anderson eagerly leaned across the desk to whisper to Marti, "I watch that show all the time. I think I was talking to that blond reporter—you know—the one who's so handsome. I'm so flustered, I can't remember his name."

Marti didn't answer. She hurried out the front door of the church offices and stood on the small porch under the overhang, stopping to wipe her eyes and blow her nose. One of Dr. Emery's dark red climbing roses trailed healthy branches over a trellis near the steps, and as she shifted the books in her arms, stuffing her damp tissue back into her handbag, a thorn from one of the branches raked her arm below the elbow. A tiny red line of blood immediately appeared, and she fished in the bag for another tissue, blotting angrily at the blood.

Darn! What else could happen?

Marti glanced across the lawn and down the empty street in front of the church. Near the far corner a light gray sedan was parked.

She gasped and instinctively stepped farther back on the porch, behind the heavy rosebush. The car was too far away for her to know if it was the same car that had followed her, and too far for her to see if someone was seated behind the wheel. If she stepped off the porch and walked down the street, would whoever was in that car try to follow her?

Marti didn't want to find out.

CHAPTER · 6

She opened the door and returned to the office. As Mrs. Anderson looked at her with surprise, Marti said, "I'll save some steps if I go out the back way," and ran down the hall to the door that exited onto the parking lot.

She hoped she hadn't been seen when she had stepped onto the porch. And she hoped that the person in the car wouldn't guess that she had left the building through another door. Marti dashed across the parking lot and down the street behind the church. Glancing over her shoulder now and then, stumbling and running, she followed another, longer route home.

There was no sign of the gray car.

Safely inside her own house, Marti went upstairs and flopped onto her bed, listening to the strong thump of her heart. *Stupid, stupid!* she blamed herself. *There are*

*lots of light gray cars. Why should you let yourself get
so scared about nothing?*

From where she lay, Marti could see the edge of
Barry's bedroom window with the blinds tightly closed,
and her longing for him was so great that she moaned
and rolled over on her stomach, curling into the ache.

"Oh, Barry," she whispered, "if you could only tell
me what happened!"

She pictured his room, the team pictures on his wall,
the tennis and Little League trophies lined up on the
top shelf of his bookcase, his bed with the battered oak
headboard, the blue-and-green-plaid bedspread, which
hung to the floor and covered everything he could stuff
under the bed each time his mother shouted, "I'm coming up to inspect. You've had enough time to clean up
that room!"

Slowly, Marti sat up as the idea grew. Maybe there
was a way that Barry could tell her what had happened.
Maybe there was something in his room that would
give her the answer. There was no reason why she
couldn't go into Barry's house to examine it. The key to
his house was downstairs in the cupboard, next to the
china, where her mother had left it.

Marti climbed off the bed and walked down the
stairs.

The key still lay in the cabinet, hard and cold in her
palm as her fingers closed around it. Marti didn't stop to
think about what she was doing. The need to see what
she could find in Barry's house was too strong. She ran
across the lawns of her house and the Logans' house, fit
the key into the lock on the Logans' front door, and
stepped inside the house, shutting the door firmly behind her. The house was dim, thermal drapes like
closed eyelids shutting out the sunlight, and its warm

mustiness smelled of loneliness and fear. For a few moments Marti stood silently, barely breathing, listening intently, feeling the horror of what had happened here closing around her.

"I have to find out," she murmured, and her words shook the silence, stirring up all the tiny popping, creaking, whispering noises that houses make. Terrified, Marti stood her ground. She had a purpose in coming here, and she was determined to carry it out.

After making sure the door was locked, Marti walked the length of the entry hall, the heels of her shoes on the tile echoing loudly. With trembling fingers she unlatched and pushed aside the louvered doors that had closed off the den, and stood in the open doorway of the room where Barry's body had been found.

The chalk markings made by the police were still visible. A half-filled glass of cola rested on the table next to one of Barry's textbooks, opened and upside down, and a videotape lay on top of the VCR. Apparently no one had disturbed this room after the police had finished their work and had gone away, but the room was not peaceful. Ragged ends of the violence that had taken place still seemed to vibrate against the windowpanes and growl in the dark corners.

Marti crossed the room quickly and raised the miniblinds. Orange-gold sunlight spilled into the room and lit the tiny motes of dust that spewed upward and slowly settled. Beyond the window were the covered patio and the pool. So many memories. Deliberately, she turned her back to the window, hugging her arms across her chest, and tried to study the room the way the police had, but nothing that she saw meant anything to her. Frustrated, she realized that she didn't know what to look for.

71

A board snapped overhead, and she looked up, startled. The house was reacting to the heat. The air conditioner would have been left on to prevent mildew and warping, but it must have been set at the high seventies.

It had been the memory of Barry's room that had triggered her decision to come here, so whatever she might find that could be helpful must be there. She dropped the miniblinds, shutting out the sunlight, and the room closed in upon itself. She fastened the louvered doors with trembling hands, locking within a murderous force so intense she had heard it, smelled it, and felt it scrape against her skin.

Across the hollow entry hall and up the carpeted stairway she walked, turned to the left, and stood at the door to Barry's room.

As she twisted the knob and pushed open the door, she stared wide-eyed, unable to believe what she saw. Each drawer in the dresser had been pulled out, its contents dumped on the floor. The bed had been torn apart, the mattress pulled askew. The closet door was wide open, and Barry's clothes had been dumped in a tangled heap.

"Why?" she groaned "Why would anyone do this?"

Someone had been here since Barry's funeral, since his parents had gone to visit relatives in San Antonio, while the house was unoccupied. Marti began to realize that this hadn't been a random trashing of Barry's things. Whoever had done this had been looking for something.

Karen. She'd call Karen.

Marti had memorized the numbers Karen had given her. She tested the telephone in Mr. and Mrs. Logan's bedroom, and found it was still connected. Good. She dialed the number of the police station, and asked for Karen. Within a few seconds Karen answered.

"What are you doing in the Logans' house?" she asked as soon as Marti told her about the state of Barry's bedroom. "Are you authorized to be there?"

"They're neighbors," Marti said. "Mrs. Logan gave Mom the key so we could bring in their mail and keep an eye on the place." She paused. "I guess we didn't do a very good job with that last part."

"All right, then," Karen said. "If you have the key and the right to be there, I'll come. It will take just a few minutes."

"Thanks," Marti said, but Karen hadn't finished.

"Marti," she said, "are you sure that you're alone in the house, that whoever was in Barry's room isn't still there?"

"I-I don't think anyone else is here," Marti answered. She turned, her back to the window, staring through the bedroom door toward the hall. She shuddered as though an ice cube had slid down her backbone.

"Just to play it safe, get out of the house. Wait for me outside, in front."

"But—"

"Do it," Karen ordered, and the conversation ended with a click.

As Marti rested the receiver on its cradle, she heard the stairs creak, then creak again, and a soft thud from the direction of Barry's room.

No one else is here, she told herself as she edged to the doorway of the bedroom and slowly, carefully, peered into the hall. *It's only the temperature changes, the settling noises a house makes.* But as a board snapped somewhere behind her, she bolted down the stairs and out the front door, dropping to the top step and hugging her knees to her chest while she shivered in the hot afternoon sunlight.

A police car took the corner quickly and halted with a screech of tires in front of the Logans' house. Karen, in uniform, hopped out and ran up the path to join Marti.

"I'll go in first," she said, and drew her gun.

Marti waited apprehensively until Karen appeared, her gun holstered. "It's okay," Karen said. "There's no sign that anyone's in the house now."

Marti led the way up the stairs and to the door of Barry's room. She stood aside to allow Karen a full view of the room. "I wonder what the person who did this was looking for," Marti said.

"First question—who was in this room?" Karen said. She turned to look at Marti. "Did you touch anything?"

"No," Marti said. "I called you right away."

"Good. I've got a kit in the car. I'll take some photos and dust for fingerprints. No telling what may turn up."

Marti kept her back to the wall, her eyes on the hall, until Karen returned, then watched while Karen busied herself around the room. She was embarrassed because there were Barry's personal things. His pajamas were draped on a chair; his favorite old Astros baseball cap with his name scrawled across it still hung on a knob on the chest of drawers.

"What are we looking for?" Marti asked.

"We don't know yet. As I work, keep your eyes open. Sometimes something is left behind. Sometimes it's taken away."

"How will we know?"

"We may not."

"Could we clean up Barry's room after you've finished? I hate to think of Mrs. Logan finding it like this."

"I'm sorry, Marti, but we can't. It's the Logans' home

that was violated, their property that was disturbed. I'll file a report on this and get the prints checked out, but I'll have to talk to them after they return home and see the room.

As Karen picked up a handful of Barry's T-shirts from the floor to see what was underneath, Marti cried out, "Oh, no! Look what they've done to Barry's photo album!"

It lay upside down where it had been thrown, some of its plastic pages caught and bent. Marti stepped forward to pick it up, but Karen snapped, "Don't touch it." Karen stooped and applied powder from her kit to the shiny brown imitation-leather cover, completing the testing for prints before she stood and said, "We got some good clear ones from that. Do you see why I told you not to touch it?"

"Yes," Marti said. "Could I look at it now?"

Karen hesitated before she wiped the cover of the album and handed it to Marti. "Memories are painful," she cautioned.

"It must be more painful *not* to have them," Marti answered.

Karen's glance was both surprised and appraising. "I'll have to give that one some thought," she said.

Marti hugged the album, carrying it to the edge of the bed, where she sat and opened it on her lap.

There was a very young, skinny, knock-kneed Barry at the beach, squinting and grinning into the sunlight, his two front teeth missing. She rapidly turned the pages, watching Barry grow older and fill out. Same grin, though. The same sense of mischievous fun consistently came through. Marti was in some of the photos. There was the one in which she wore her first formal. Pink taffeta. Ninth grade, wasn't it? Her fingertips grazed the edge of the photograph. *Oh, Barry,* she thought, *I didn't know you had kept this picture.*

The photos were of Barry in high school now, but there were gaps on the pages, and some of the photographs were out of alignment. "Karen," Marti said, "there are some pictures missing from this album."

Karen sat beside her and turned a couple of the pages. "They weren't removed neatly," she said. "Whoever did it was in a hurry."

"Why would he do it?"

"The person who did it had a reason. It's up to us to find out what it was."

"How? We don't even know what pictures he took."

Karen climbed off the bed. "Maybe you do. Go through the whole album," she said. "Guess what might be missing. That may be our only clue."

Her heart aching, Marti scanned the rest of the pages. Barry in his tennis whites, Barry getting a trophy, Barry smiling at the judges, Barry and that brunette airhead in the eleventh grade. What was her name? Barbie? Barry had lost interest in that girl in a hurry, and Marti was glad. He was much too good for her.

She closed the book and tried to think. "All that's in here is a collection of photos of Barry and his friends." Marti suddenly clapped a hand over her mouth and gasped. "Except for the Cuatros!" she cried.

Fumbling in her eagerness, she flipped through the pages of the album again and looked up at Karen in triumph. "There should be a lot of pictures of the Cuatros in this book because they were always taking pictures of themselves, but there aren't any. Someone's removed all of them."

"Do you have copies of any of the missing photos?"

"No, but Charlie and Tony ought to. I can ask them." She stood up and carefully placed the album on Barry's bed. "Or Mrs. Miller."

Karen snapped the lock on the small case she'd brought in and looked at Marti. "Mrs. Miller? Who's she?"

"Thad's mother. His family lives in Farrington Park."

"I thought you told me they had moved away."

Marti shook her head. "No, I just said that *Thad* didn't live here anymore."

Karen glanced at her sharply. "Are we playing guessing games? Is there some reason why Thad left and his family didn't?"

Marti shrugged, uncomfortable at having to talk about it. "Two years ago Thad was convicted of armed robbery and sent to a juvenile detention center near Martinglen."

"Why didn't you tell me this earlier?"

"I didn't think it was important." Marti shifted from one foot to the other and looked down, not wanting to meet Karen's eyes.

Karen was silent for a moment, then said, "I think you'd better start at the beginning and tell me this whole story about Thad—and the other Cuatros."

At this Marti's head snapped up. "The others had nothing to do with the robbery. Thad was wild. He always wanted to do something daring or crazy, and most of the time the other guys would go along, like the time when Thad dared them all to jump off the railroad trestle over the Brazos when it was swollen after a big rain, and Tony almost drowned, and—"

She stopped, unaccountably shivering, then said, "This time Thad wanted to rob a store. He really didn't care what kind of a store, but he finally settled on a

77

small jewelry store—the one in that little shopping center that faces the freeway. Thad's plan was for all the Cuatros to wear ski masks and wait until there weren't any customers and burst in and grab watches and diamond rings and stuff and get out fast."

As she stopped for breath, Karen asked, "Did the others go along with it?"

"No!" Marti said. "They tried to talk Thad out of it. They told him he was crazy. They thought they'd changed his mind."

"He committed the robbery alone?"

"Yes. And it went the way he planned it, except that when he tried to sell the things he took at a pawn shop, the shop owner turned him in to the police. Thad tried to pretend it was just a prank, sort of like a hazing stunt, but nobody believed him."

"Why was that?"

Marti took a deep breath before she answered. "Because Barry, Charlie, and Tony—the other Cuatros—all testified against him."

CHAPTER · 7

Marti walked with Karen to her car. "They felt terrible about it," Marti said. "Barry even cried when he told me they'd be called by the prosecuting attorney to testify. But they had to tell the truth." She paused, then asked, "Are you going to talk to Charlie and Tony?"

"Yes," Karen said, "but not now. I'm on duty, and—as I told you—this isn't a case we're supposed to be working. I'll get to Barry's friends as soon as I can manage it. I do have questions for them, and there are other questions I'll have to find answers for."

"I could help you."

Karen nodded. "With Tony and Charlie, yes, but some of the information I need will be easy to get through routine procedures." She climbed into the car and shut the door, but before putting her key in the

79

ignition, Karen rolled down the window in her door and called, "Marti? There *is* something you could tell me."

"Sure," Marti said. She hurried to the driver's side of the car and bent toward the window. "What is it?"

"You said Thad was convicted of armed robbery. Offhand, do you remember what kind of a gun he used?"

"Thad claimed it was a toy gun—a water pistol, but the jewelry-store owner said he knew the gun was real. He was just too upset to pay attention to what kind of gun it was."

Karen gave an impatient toss of her head. "Didn't they have the gun for evidence? Where was the gun?"

"Thad said he'd thrown it into one of the bayous. He didn't remember where. No one ever found it."

"Was it possible that it really wasn't a toy? That it had been owned by his parents?"

"No. They claimed they had never owned a gun."

Karen looked so dubious that Marti felt defensive. "It could have been a toy gun," she said.

"Yes, it could," Karen admitted.

"There are so many questions." Marti sighed.

"I'm used to questions," Karen said. "The ones I don't like are the ones without answers."

She brushed back the short red ringlets that were damp against her cheeks and moved to roll up the window, but Marti cried, "Wait! Talking about guns has made me think of something. What happened to the gun they found with Barry?"

"I don't know offhand. It was sent to HPD Ballistics for testing. If the Logans want it back, it will probably be given to them."

"It wasn't the Logans' gun," Marti said. The sun scorched through her thin shirt, and drops of sweat rolled down her backbone. The side of the car was hot where she leaned against it. "Mrs. Logan's afraid of guns. She never wanted one in the house."

"Barry's, then?"

"No," Marti said. "I know for sure that Barry never owned a gun."

"I'll find out if they traced the one that was found," Karen said.

"When?"

"You'll have to be patient. I'll do this when I can."

Marti straightened, taking a step away from the car. "Thanks for helping me, Karen. I appreciate it. I really do."

"You don't need to thank me. It's part of my job to investigate, to try to find the truth."

"But you're doing this as a favor to me."

Karen shook her head. "No," she said. "I'm doing it because if there's even a particle of doubt that Barry didn't kill himself, then I have the responsibility to look for the truth."

"Thanks," Marti whispered. Tears rushed to her eyes, and Karen's face became a blur.

"We're going to have a tough job, partner," Karen said, "and we may never be successful in proving our case, but we'll try."

Karen rolled up the window and started the ignition. Marti watched her drive away. She rubbed the back of one hand across her eyes and went into the house to start dinner. *Partner,* Karen had called her. She liked that. Well, there was one thing this half of the partnership could do—and do this evening, as soon as dinner was over. She was going to Charlie's house and ask to see his pictures of the Cuatros.

81

* * *

Charlie started when he opened the door and saw Marti. "What do you want?" he asked, a frown creasing a V between his eyebrows.

"Is that your polite way of inviting me in?" Marti leaned against the doorframe and stared up at him.

"Cut out the sarcasm," he grumbled. "It's just that you didn't call or anything. I wasn't expecting you."

"So?"

For a moment Charlie looked puzzled, until Marti said, "I'm here, whether you want me to be or not. Aren't you going to ask me in?"

Charlie looked up the street, which was empty except for a few cars parked in driveways, and moved back to make room for Marti to pass. "I'm sorry, Marti," he said. "I've got a lot on my mind."

"And you were expecting somebody."

He whirled to face her. "It's not what you think."

"How do you know what I think?"

"Look, Mom and Dad are in Houston tonight. They went to a play at the Alley Theater. It just seemed like a good time to get in some extra studying, so I asked—uh —somebody to come over."

Marti followed Charlie to the den and plopped onto an upholstered rocker. "Who is she?"

"It doesn't matter," Charlie mumbled. He went to the telephone on the bar counter that separated the den from the kitchen and dialed a number. His voice was low, but Marti could pick up the words "Later. Call you back."

"I don't know why it's such a big secret," Marti said. "Is it that tall, blond girl who just moved here from California? I've noticed her noticing you."

Charlie sat on the sofa across from Marti and leaned

forward, forearms resting on his legs, his hands clasped in front of him. "I thought you didn't want to talk. You didn't want to hear what I had to say after lit class."

Marti tried to smile. "Let's start over. We're both having a lot of trouble getting our lives back together. I'm sorry I was rude to you today. That's one reason I'm here."

"It's okay, I guess." Charlie kept his eyes on her. "It depends on what the other reason is."

"I'd like to see your photograph album."

He looked bewildered, as though he'd expected something else. "I haven't got an album," he answered.

"You have pictures, don't you?"

"Sure. But I toss them all in a big box. I never did get around to putting an album together."

"It doesn't matter, as long as you've got photographs of the Cuatros."

Charlie sat upright, and suspicion narrowed his eyes. "What do you want the photographs for?"

Marti stood, crossed the space between them, and sat next to Charlie. She took one of his hands. "Because of Barry, we've been friends for a long time," she said, "and now we're acting like enemies. I don't know why you mistrust me, and I don't want you to, so I'm going to be very open with you and tell you what I know."

She described the way she'd found Barry's room and told him how Karen had taken photos and fingerprints and how she, Marti, had looked through Barry's album and found all the pictures of the Cuatros were missing.

During the telling, Charlie's fingers had been tense in hers, but at that point he pulled his hand away and shifted position so that he ended up a few inches away from her. "Do you know who took them?" he asked.

Marti shook her head.

"Or why?" His voice was low, as if he were talking to himself. "Why the Cuatros?" He suddenly put his head down in his hands and groaned. "It makes everything worse." he said.

"I don't understand," Marti said.

He slowly sat up and looked at her, his features twisted with pain. "That's right. You don't. And all this stupid playing detective, insisting that Barry was murdered . . . why can't you just back off and accept things the way they are?"

"You can't understand *me,*" Marti said. "I wonder if you even understood Barry."

"Of course I did!" Charlie shouted at her. "We were close friends! Don't you think that when he killed himself it tore me apart?"

"I keep telling you—he didn't kill himself."

"Who would kill him?"

"I don't know!" Marti found that she was shouting too. She flung herself against the back of the sofa, slumping, her chin almost on her chest, and quietly asked, "Charlie, why are we doing this to each other?"

"Because you won't let go."

They were silent for a few moments, until the silence became oppressive, pounding at her ears. Marti broke it. "Could I see your photographs?"

Charlie rested his elbows on his knees again and put his forehead into the palms of his hands. "I don't know where they are," he mumbled.

"They have to be somewhere around here. I'll help you look."

His words were deliberately spaced, as though he were talking to a child who couldn't understand. "I . . . don't . . . know . . . where . . . they . . . are."

The house was cool with air-conditioning, but Marti

The house was cool with air-conditioning, but Marti saw beads of sweat popping out on Charlie's forehead and on his hands. "You've thought of something, haven't you? What are you afraid of?" she asked.

His voice was a hollow whisper as he raised his head to stare into her eyes. "Right now," he said, "I'm afraid of you."

Charlie's house was on the street behind Castle Lake Drive, but Tony's wasn't within walking distance; so Marti walked home in the darkness, puzzling over what Charlie had said. It didn't make sense. She sighed. Maybe Karen could figure it out.

Once inside the house she went to the telephone in her bedroom and dialed Tony's number.

Busy. She should have known. The minute she left Charlie he had probably telephoned Tony. She waited a few minutes and dialed again, but the number was still busy. She sighed. Wait five minutes, then dial again. If she still couldn't get Tony, she'd call the Millers.

She didn't want to talk to Mrs. Miller. She could still remember the woman's face, so stiff-lipped and pale when she and Mom met her in the supermarket after the trial and Mom tried to say something comforting about Thad. But how about Thad's brother, Emmet? They never had much to say to each other in lit. class, but she didn't mind calling Emmet.

Emmet was the one who answered the phone, which Marti thought would make things easier, but after she had identified herself, Emmet just mumbled, "Yeah?"

Marti decided to get right to the point. "Emmet," she said, "if you have any photographs of the Cuatros, I'd like to have them."

He made a quick, explosive sound. His words were so

85

garbled she couldn't understand them. "Emmet?" she
asked. "Did you hear me?"

"I heard you," he grumbled. "What makes you think
I'd want pictures of those guys?"

"Well, I didn't mean *you*, exactly. I really meant photographs that belong to Thad. Does he have an album
or a box of photos, anything like that?"

"You've got to be kidding. He trashed them. Burned
them up, as a matter of fact."

Marti gasped. "But the Cuatros were friends."

"Friends? That's what you call them? None of them
stood by him. They couldn't even tell a couple of white
lies that would have kept Thad from getting that sentence."

"They were under oath. They couldn't lie."

"They were as guilty as Thad was," he snapped.
"Thad did it as a joke, and the guys knew he was going
to do it. They could have stopped him, but they didn't;
so he had to prove he could do it."

"You're wrong!" Marti began, but Emmet had hung
up.

The telephone rang the moment she pressed down
the button to break the circuit. She jumped and held
the receiver away from her body as though it were a
live thing.

"Hello? Hello?" she heard.

Marti gulped and brought the phone to her ear.
"Hello," she answered.

A woman's voice asked, "May I please speak to Marti
Lewis?"

Marti recognized Miss Dillard's voice and grimaced
into the phone. "This is Marti."

The voice picked up speed and volume. "Well, Marti,
this is Elizabeth Dillard. Didn't you get my note? I

waited for fifteen minutes after class, but you didn't show up."

"I had another appointment, Miss Dillard. With Dr. Emery."

"Then it was my fault in assuming you'd be free."

Marti didn't answer, and after an awkward pause, Miss Dillard asked, "Will you be able to meet with me tomorrow after class?"

"Tomorrow is Friday."

"I know how all of you kids are about Fridays and getting away for the weekends, but Dr. Granberry is eager to meet you. He's very interested in what you told me about Barry. I promise that we won't keep you long."

For a moment it was hard to breathe, and Marti could feel her heart beat faster. "You mean he's interested in what I said about Barry not killing himself?"

"Oh. Oh, no." Miss Dillard began to apologize. "I mean what you said about Barry's lack of depression and all his plans for the future, and so forth. You know there are so many studies being made right now, so much need for input and information, and I feel that Dr. Granberry's on the right track, that the information he puts together could be of immense help to so many families of troubled young people."

"He's dealing with suicides. Barry's death wasn't a suicide."

Miss Dillard's voice was strained. "Please, Marti. Dr. Granberry just wants to talk to you, and he's asked me as a favor to arrange it. Please? I think a meeting will be of benefit to you both."

"Okay," Marti said, and let out a long sigh. "I'll be in your office after school tomorrow."

"Thank you," Miss Dillard told her. "I know this is hard for you, and I really do appreciate your help."

As Marti hung up the phone her mother called from the foot of the stairs, "Marti? Are you off the telephone yet?"

Marti went into the upper hall and leaned over the railing. She looked at her watch, amazed at the time. "I didn't know how late it was. I haven't started dinner yet."

"Don't worry about it. We've sent out for pizza. You've been on the phone so long, a couple of calls came for you on our line. Kim, for one. Were you supposed to go there for dinner?"

"Oh, no! I forgot about Kim." Marti groaned.

"Well, there's another call waiting right now. Better pick up the phone in our bedroom. It's someone named Karen Prescott. She said that she'd been trying to get you, but your line has been busy. She's on the phone now. Marti?"

But Marti was already running down the hall to her parents' room. She snatched up the receiver and said, "Karen? I'm sorry I was on the phone for so long."

"It's all right," Karen said. "I stayed late tonight, and I'm ready to drive back to Houston, which is why I tried your parents' number. Before I leave the office, I want to give you some information."

"About what?"

"Just listen. It's about Thad Miller. Two weeks ago he was released on parole from the juvenile detention center."

Marti gripped the phone so tightly that her knuckles ached. "Where is he now?"

"That's the problem," Karen told her. "At this moment, I don't know."

CHAPTER · 8

For a few minutes after their conversation had ended, Marti stood by her parents' bed, staring down at the telephone. Her stomach churned and fury rose in hot waves, burning her chest, scalding her cheeks. She stomped to her own room, looked up the Millers' phone number again, and dialed. Emmet answered.

"Where's your brother?" Marti demanded.

"What are you talking about?"

"Don't play dumb. A police officer just told me that Thad was released from the detention center two weeks ago."

There was a moment of silence before Emmet asked, "How come the police told you that? What have you got to do with anything?"

"I told the police that Barry didn't commit suicide."

"Yeah. After what you said in assembly, I guess you would."

With embarrassment Marti remembered the scene she had made. "Barry was murdered. I know it."

"So you said. That's real dumb. Going to the police was even dumber. They aren't going to help you."

"Then *you* help me. Tell me where Thad is."

Emmet chuckled, and the sound was so smug and mocking that Marti shuddered. "If you think you can stick Thad with anything, you're crazy. Thad's with Mom and Dad. They took him to a place near Austin. He's going to live with one of our uncles on his cattle ranch. He's got an alibi—has he ever!—for anything you might dream up."

Marti couldn't help feeling disturbed, no matter what Emmet had told her. "You're sure of this, Emmet?"

"You asked me a question. I answered it. Stop bugging me," he said, and slammed down the phone.

I don't believe him, Marti thought. *He's lying to protect his brother.* The more she thought about it, the more she was sure. There was something odd in Emmet's voice that snaked through the hostility and smugness. Emmet knew more than he had told her. Emmet was hiding something.

Marti dialed Tony's number. Still busy.

She called Kim. "I'm sorry," Marti said the moment Kim answered. "I got busy. I forgot I was coming over. I forgot everything."

"Were you talking to Dr. Emery all that time?"

"No," Marti said, "but other things came up. "Can I fill you in later? Please?"

As soon as Kim reluctantly agreed, Marti said a quick good-bye, snatched up her shoulder bag and car keys, and ran down the stairs. "Could I borrow the car?" she called into the den, where her parents were watching a situation comedy on television. She could hear bursts of canned laughter from the set.

"Don't you want some pizza?" her father called.

Her mother shouted, "It's after eight o'clock. Where are you going?"

"To Tony's house. I won't be long. I've just got to pick up something. And I'm not hungry. Really."

Marti could hear a low murmur of voices as her parents talked to each other. "It's better that she's out and busy than up in her room brooding," she heard her father say. Her mother murmured something, which was drowned out by another loud burst of television laughter. Then her father called, "Take the car, Marti, but don't stay out too late."

For an instant Marti felt a little dizzy with the strange feeling that none of them were real; that her parents weren't in the den, and she wasn't in the hall, and only their computerized voices were bouncing back and forth through an empty house, being mixed and matched with the canned laughter from the television set by ghostly hands on ghostly dials.

But what she had to do was real. Very real.

Marti drove to Tony's house and rang the bell. His mother opened the door and greeted Marti warmly.

"I tried to call first, but the line was busy," Marti explained.

"I'm afraid that's my fault," Mrs. Lopez told her. "I'm trying to line up a committee for our annual Prevent Child Abuse fund raiser. You wouldn't believe how many calls it takes!"

"Has Charlie been here?"

"No," Mrs. Lopez said, "but he did phone Tony a few

minutes ago, and I guess he'd had the same trouble trying to get through that you had." She laughed. "Well, most of the time it's teenagers hogging the phone. Mothers have a right to take a turn once in a while too."

Marti smiled. "Where is Tony?"

"He's in the library," his mother said. The telephone rang and she turned toward the sound, saying over her shoulder, "I hope that's Helen Schaeffer, returning my call. You know where the library is, Marti. You might lend Tony a hand. The last time I saw him, he was looking through all the things in those covered cabinets, trying to find his photo album."

Marti ran down the hall and burst into the paneled library, startling Tony, who was seated cross-legged on the floor, his album on his lap, a stack of photographs scattered on the rug near him. He wasn't wearing a shirt, so his well-developed chest and arm muscles gleamed in the lamplight. Tony was the strongest of the Cuatros, Marti knew, and the scowl he turned on her was menacing.

"What are you doing here?" he snapped.

He made a dive for the loose photographs, but Marti was faster. She scooped up most of them and whirled out of his reach. "Here they are. The Cuatros," she said, thumbing through them.

"Give those back!" Tony demanded as he scrambled to his feet.

Marti held the photographs behind her and quickly backed to the open doorway. "What did Charlie tell you to do with these pictures?" she asked.

"They're my pictures. I have a right to do whatever I want with them."

Marti heard footsteps, and from the corner of her eye

saw Mrs. Lopez coming to join them. Marti raised her voice. "You're going to destroy these, aren't you?"

"So what if I am? It's none of your business." Tony moved toward her. "Give them to me."

"No!" Marti cried out in pain as he grabbed her arm. "These are pictures of Barry! If you don't want them, why can't I have them?"

Tony's eyes narrowed. "What's the big act for? I know why you—"

But his mother hurried forward and put an arm around Marti's shoulders. "For goodness' sake, what are you doing, Tony? Let go of Marti. You're hurting her!"

Tony guiltily dropped Marti's arm and backed away. "It's nothing, Mom. Don't look like that. We were just— just kidding around."

"That didn't look like kidding around to me," she said. "One of you tell me. What's this all about?"

Marti held out the photographs to Mrs. Lopez. She rubbed her arm, which still hurt where Tony had gripped it. "These are pictures of the Cuatros. Barry is in them. Tony took them out of his album because he's going to throw them away, but I want them. I don't want these pictures of Barry to be destroyed."

Mrs. Lopez frowned at her son. "I certainly don't blame you, Marti. And I don't understand Tony at all. Why in the world would you want to destroy these photographs?"

"I dunno, Mom," Tony mumbled. "It made me feel awful to look at them. I guess I just didn't want them around."

Mrs. Lopez scanned through the photographs. When she finished there were tears in her eyes. "Such fine boys. But such a tragedy. So much sadness. Two of them—" She handed the photographs to Marti and stepped into the room, putting her arms around Tony. "Son," she said softly, "I can understand how much pain you must feel when you look at these pictures, but if Marti wants them and you don't, then there's no reason you shouldn't give them to her. Is there?"

"I guess not," Tony said, but he glared at Marti over his mother's shoulder.

"Thank you, Mrs. Lopez. Thank you, Tony," Marti said meekly, and hurried from the house before Tony could come up with a way to get his hands on those photographs.

When Marti entered her own house, she called out, "I'm home," and two voices answered at the same time, "That's nice, dear," and "Okay, hon."

"Oh, by the way," her mother added, "Charlie telephoned. I told him you'd call him back the minute you got home."

Marti gripped the knob on the post at the foot of the stairs. "I don't want to talk to Charlie right now, Mom. If he calls back, tell him I'll see him tomorrow. Okay?"

She took the stairs at a gallop, shut her bedroom door, and spread out the two dozen or so photographs on her desk under the bright lamp. Aching with loneliness, she stared at Barry in the photographs, not wanting to look at anyone or anything else. "I miss you," she whispered, and tears filled her eyes.

She forced herself to tear her thoughts away from Barry and to study the photos intently; but she could find nothing. There were pictures of the guys in bathing suits at Surfside, at school, and around Tony's red sports car—Barry in his ever present beat-up Astros baseball cap. There was even an oversized school photo of the Cuatros in the Western desperado costumes they had worn two years ago for that crazy talent-show act they'd dreamed up. She was in three of the pictures, Emmet in one. In a few, other kids in school had posed with them. A handful of the photos included only three of the Cuatros, with one probably taking the photograph; but most of the photos showed the four Cuatros together, and she looked at these with the most care.

Nothing.

The phone rang, but she ignored it.

Marti shoved back her chair and tried to think. What was she looking for? What could there be in one or more of these pictures that someone didn't want her— or anyone else—to see?

The telephone rang again persistently, but the moment the caller had hung up Marti took the receiver off its stand. She did not want to talk to Charlie.

One by one, Marti picked up the photographs again, studying each with care, going over all the details. Here was a shot taken at the beach. Thad was holding a surfboard. Behind them, unaware of the camera, strolled two girls in bikinis. As the photo was taken, Charlie had turned, looking over his shoulder at the girls. Were these girls significant in any way? She shook her head. Just to Charlie.

Next photo. The group around Tony's car. Anything important here? Tony was in the driver's seat, hands on the wheel, Barry leaning on the hood, a big grin on his face, his Astros cap pulled down over his eyes. Again, Marti shook her head.

By the time she reached the last picture she was exhausted, but she went through the same routine. Here were the four in their desperado costumes. Thad in a white felt Western hat with a wide brim. Thad was holding a kid's stick horse. Tony was leaning on Charlie.

Barry was wearing a black Stetson, his left arm across his chest, a gun in his hand.

A gun in his hand?

She squinted at the handgun he was holding across his chest, his finger on the trigger. She guessed the barrel to be about six inches long. Surely it was a toy gun. It had to be. But there was something about its size and shape that made her wonder.

"Mom!" she called as she reached the top of the stairs and hung over the railing, "Where's that magnifying glass you bought so you could read the Houston city maps?"

"In the top drawer of my desk," Mom shouted back.

"Thanks!" Marti ran downstairs to the room, which had been outfitted with twin desks for her parents—a spillover office for work that had to be continued at home—and rummaged in the top drawer of her mother's desk until she found the magnifying glass. Clutching it, she raced back up the stairs to her own desk.

Marti slowly moved the glass upward and downward over the picture of the gun, studying it carefully. She tried to remember the bulky cap pistols with their shiny chrome barrels and the fat black plastic water pistols—the toy guns. None of them had the slender sleekness of the gun in Barry's hand. No. She was sure that he had been holding a real gun.

Shaken, she dropped the magnifying glass on the desk and leaned back in her chair. Barry with a gun? Is this what Charlie and Tony were trying to keep from her?

"Oh, Barry!" She moaned, then whispered, "I thought you told me nearly everything. Why didn't you tell me you owned a gun?"

The answer popped into her head: *Maybe it wasn't Barry's gun.*

"Then whose was it?" she asked.

The Cuatros know.

Marti wrapped her arms tightly around herself, hugging her shoulders, and looked out at the starless black void that had swallowed Barry's house. She'd telephone Karen and tell her what she had found. Karen would know what do do next.

A deep voice answered the phone, and Marti was taken aback. "I-I-maybe I have the wrong number. That is, I-I wanted to speak to Karen Prescott."

"You've got the right number," the voice said. "Hang on. She'll be with you in a minute."

When Karen answered Marti began apologizing. "I guess I shouldn't have called so late. I didn't mean to interrupt you."

"It's not that late," Karen said. "And I know you wouldn't call if it weren't important. What's on your mind?"

Marti told her about the photograph and what she had gone through to get it.

"The photo may or may not have any significance," Karen said, "but it's probably a good idea to get it out of your hands."

"Do you want me to take it to you? Right now?"

"No. I'll call the station and get whoever's on duty to pick it up. Just put the picture in an envelope with my name on it, seal it, and stand by. An officer will be at your house in a few minutes. I'll take a look at it when I get to the station tomorrow."

"Okay," Marti said.

As soon as she had hung up, she did as Karen told her, tucked the small envelope in her shirt pocket, and ran downstairs. "Marti," her mother said as they came face-to-face at the foot of the stairs, "I thought you were in bed."

"I had some stuff to do," Marti told her.

"It's late, and you have school tomorrow."

"I'll be upstairs in just a couple of minutes. I promise."

Her father turned out the last downstairs light and joined them, giving Marti a fond smile. "I remember when I was young. I could think of a dozen things to do rather than go to bed," he said.

The doorbell rang so suddenly that the three of them started, her mother giving a little gasp.

"Oh, no," Marti groaned. She'd been hoping to avoid this by watching for the officer and handing him the envelope with no one the wiser. Now there'd be explanations for hours.

Her father turned on the outside light and opened the door. To Marti's surprise, Charlie and Tony stood there.

"I know it's late," Charlie said before either of her parents could say a word, "but we need to talk to Marti. Could we come in?"

Marti's mother pointedly looked at her watch, but her father held the door open wide and said, "Come in, boys. You're always welcome here. Come in, come in."

"We won't be long," Tony mumbled. His glance shifted from the floor to the wall and to a place over their heads. He didn't meet her father's eyes.

No one but Marti seemed to notice.

"We'll say good night," her father told them, and began to climb the stairs.

"Remember, it's already late," her mother chided,

but smiled to soften the message, and followed her husband up the stairs.

Marti led Tony and Charlie into the nearest room—the living room—and turned on one of the floor lamps. She positioned herself by the window, where she could see the street.

For a moment Tony and Charlie stood next to each other, looking uncomfortable, neither of them speaking.

"Which one of you trashed Barry's room and stole the pictures from his album?" Marti asked, her voice bitter.

"You think we did it?" Tony muttered. He dropped into the nearest chair and slumped, his chin on his chest.

"We wouldn't do a thing like that," Charlie told her. "You should know that, Marti."

"Then who did it?"

They both looked right into her eyes. "We don't know," Charlie said. "We wish we did."

She didn't know whether to believe them or not, and it disturbed her to think that they might be lying to her. "Then what's all this stuff you're doing about hiding the photographs, trying to destroy them before anybody sees them?"

Tony looked at Charlie, and Charlie said, "We have our reasons. Marti, give Tony back the pictures you took."

"You'll have to do better than that," Marti said. She saw headlights from a car and watched from the corner of her eye as it pulled up in front of her house. It was a marked patrol car.

"Why should we?" Charlie's voice had an edge sharpened by anger or fear. Marti couldn't tell which. She couldn't figure out what was the matter with Charlie.

"You conned Tony's mom and got something that didn't belong to you," Charlie said. "All we're asking is that you give it back."

A uniformed officer got out of the car and began to walk toward the Lewises' front door. Marti edged past Charlie and walked into the entry hall.

Charlie took a step back, surprise on his face. "Where are you going?" he asked.

Marti didn't answer. She opened the front door just before the officer reached it.

"Marti Lewis?" the officer asked.

"Yes," she said. She pulled the envelope from her pocket and held it out. As he took it she added, "Thanks."

"Sure," he answered. "No problem. I'll put this on Officer Prescott's desk. She'll get it first thing tomorrow morning." As he began to walk back to his car, Marti shut the door.

She turned to see Tony and Charlie staring at her from the doorway to the living room.

"What did you just do?" Tony whispered. Charlie's face sagged, and he looked as ill as if someone had punched him in the stomach.

Marti walked past them into the living room and sat on the brocade sofa. "I gave him one of the photographs," she said. "The one in which the Cuatros are dressed like Western desperados. The one in which Barry's holding a gun. The officer who's helping me thinks it's worth checking into."

Tony sat on the nearest chair and closed his eyes.

"Oh, Marti." Charlie dropped beside her on the sofa. His lips moved as though he were trying to speak, but instead he leaned over and rested his head in his hands.

Charlie's shoulders shook, and Marti realized that he was crying.

Apprehensively, Marti said, "I've been truthful with both of you, and you haven't been with me. What's this all about? Why won't you tell me? It's that gun in the photograph, isn't it?"

"Yes," Tony said.

Charlie raised his head and looked at her. His face was blotchy and red. He pulled a handkerchief out of his pocket and loudly blew his nose. "One of the pictures in the *Houston Post* showed the gun found next to Barry's body," he said. "The picture was clear enough so that we knew it was the same gun as the one in that desperados photograph."

Marti heard the words, but it took a moment before they registered. "Are you telling me that was Barry's gun?" she whispered.

"No," Charlie said. "It's mine."

CHAPTER · 9

Marti could only stare at Charlie. For a moment thoughts exploded and bounced inside her head like flashes of light. She'd reach out to grasp them, but they'd slip through her fingers. "Charlie?" she stammered. "Charlie . . . you didn't—"

"I didn't give the gun to Barry," he said.

She leaned forward, her fingers digging into the upholstered seat of the sofa. "Who did you give it to?"

"I didn't give it to anybody! When I saw what looked like our gun in that newspaper photograph I-I went right to the place where we'd hidden it, only the gun wasn't there. I don't know who took it."

"You told me it was *your* gun. Now you're saying, *our* gun."

"It doesn't matter. I'm just trying to explain that—"

"It *does* matter," Marty insisted. "Whoever took that gun killed Barry."

103

"Will you get off it!" Charlie snapped. "The police—
even the medical examiner—said Barry committed suicide. All this snooping around you're doing is making
everything worse."

Marti edged back, away from Charlie. His fear was a
damp, crawly thing, and she couldn't let it touch her.
"Did you have something to do with Barry's death?"
she demanded. "Why are you trying so hard to cover up
the gun?"

His eyes widened, and he stammered, "N-now wait a
minute, Marti. Don't start thinking that I—"

"What are you trying to keep from me?"

"I'm not. I—"

"Is it Thad? Have you been in contact with him since
he was released?"

Tony jumped to his feet. "Thad's out? Since when?"

Charlie's eyes were glazed glass in a chalk-white face
as he stared at Marti.

"You didn't know, did you?" Marti said.

Charlie turned his head stiffly and looked up at Tony.
"Do you think—" His voice creaked to a stop.

"If he came back—"

"You're talking around me," Marti complained. "It's
not fair. There are things you know that I should be
told."

Tony lowered himself to a chair at Marti's other side.
"Maybe we should tell her," he said to Charlie. "You do
it. Start at the beginning. Tell Marti the whole thing."

Charlie let out a long sigh and leaned over, his forearms resting on his thighs. His knuckles, protruding
from tightly twisted fingers, were bloodless knobs, and
his voice was low. Marti strained to hear.

"It was when we were putting together that desperado skit, back when we were all in the tenth grade,"

Charlie said. "I got a water pistol to use for the gun, but Thad said it didn't look right. He thought it would be funny if we used a real gun because Old Billingsly would have a screaming fit if he knew we were up there onstage with a real gun. The big joke was that nobody would know but us. Barry thought it was a great idea and agreed with Thad that we should do it. Tony did too."

"We *all* did," Tony muttered.

"So we drove into Houston and went to a couple of pawnshops," Charlie said, "but they turned us down because we were only sixteen. We went to an awful run-down neighborhood, where some guys were sitting outside a bar and we asked them if they knew somebody who'd sell us a gun, and they just laughed at us. But one guy followed us down the street to the car and told us he'd come up with a gun for us if we'd make it worth his while. He got in the car with us and directed us to a pawnshop a couple of blocks away. He sat on the front seat between Barry and me—I was driving—and wanted to know our names and what we were going to do with the gun—things like that. Barry made up a name and a lot of crazy stuff. I could tell that the guy knew Barry was lying."

"How about you?" Marti asked. "What did you tell him?"

"Like a fool, I had already told him my name. I wish I hadn't."

Charlie shuddered as though he were shaking off the memories, and went on. "When we parked in front of the shop the guy asked us how much money we had and said it was barely enough to buy a gun, but he'd see what he could do. He took the money into the shop, and we watched through the window while he bought the gun. In a few minutes he came out and handed it to us. Thad complained that the gun should have been a larger size. The one the guy bought for us was a .22 and kind of small for Western desperados, but he said that was the best we could get for the money. I think the creep pocketed most of it."

Marti interrupted. "You were lucky to get anything. How could you all have been so dumb as to give that stranger your money? I'm surprised he didn't just go out the back door of the shop with it."

"We know all that. We realized at the time we were being stupid." He scowled at her. "Didn't you ever do anything stupid and wished you hadn't?"

"Of course I have," Marti said. She touched his shoulder in sympathy. "I guess sooner or later everybody does. I didn't mean to interrupt. Go on."

Charlie gave her a last reproachful glance, then continued. "The guy left, so we went into the shop to see if we could change the gun for something that looked more Western, but the shop owner said no. And while Thad was trying to argue him into it, Tony and I looked down at the handgun register that was still lying open on the counter. The guy who'd bought the gun for us had used *my* name. He'd registered the gun to *me*!"

"How could he do that?" Marti asked.

"I don't know," Charlie said, "but he did it. He'd given a different address from mine and hadn't put down a phone number. I guess the shop owner hadn't asked for ID. Maybe he even knew the guy."

"It could have been their own private joke," Tony said.

Marti looked from one to the other. "Didn't you say anything about it to the shop owner?"

Tony shook his head. "He just kept yelling at us and

106

tried to get us out of there in a hurry. He was a real big guy, and mean. We were all scared of him."

"We did use the gun in the skit," Charlie said. He dropped his voice again. "Knowing it was a real gun wasn't that funny. We kept remembering those guys in Houston."

"Barry didn't tell me any of that," Marti said slowly, as though she were thinking aloud.

Charlie looked at her sharply. "Would you have told anybody? Do you have any idea how stupid we felt?"

"I guess not," Marti said. She thought a moment. "You said you put the gun away after the talent show was over."

"That's right," Tony said. "We hid it in the back of the closet in Charlie's bedroom."

"Have you got any idea who took it from the hiding place?"

Charlie's voice was filled with misery. "It had to be Barry, didn't it?"

"No. It didn't. Didn't all four of you know where the gun was hidden?"

"Hey, wait a minute!" Tony exploded. "Do you think that Charlie or I—"

Marti shook her head impatiently as she interrupted. "Are you positive that nobody touched that gun since your desperados skit?"

Charlie looked down and didn't answer.

Finally Tony urged, "Tell her, Charlie. Tell her the rest of it."

Mom suddenly appeared in the doorway. She was wrapped in her pink cotton robe and had a couple of rollers in the front of her hair. Her eyes, bare of makeup, looked older and puffy. "I know I sound like a grouch," she said, "but enough is enough. It's *very* late,

107

and you all have school tomorrow. I'm going to have to ask you to leave now, Tony . . . Charlie."

"Mom!" Marti said. "This is important!"

"Not as important as a good night's sleep," she answered. "Good night, boys."

Tony stood up. Charlie followed, and they walked toward the door.

"I have to hear all of the story," Marti told them.

Charlie nodded. "Meet at my house tomorrow right after school. Don't take too long, because I'm working a five P.M. shift at the Jumbo Burger."

"I can be there," Tony said.

"Wait!" They paused on the porch and Marti squeezed past her mother, who was trying to shut the front door. "I've got to meet with Miss Dillard right after school, but it won't take much time. I promise. Just wait for me. I'll get there as soon as I can."

"Okay," Charlie said as Marti's mother shut the door.

She turned to face Marti. The hope in her eyes was so obvious that Marty felt guilty. "What's this about a meeting with Miss Dillard?" she asked. "Did you decide to go to her for counseling after all?"

"No, Mom," Marti said. "She wants me to meet Clement Granberry. He's that psychologist she's going to work with in writing the book."

Her mother's forehead puckered as she remembered. "If this is something you'd rather not do, Marti—"

"It's okay," Marti said. She put an arm around her mother's shoulders, suddenly thinking about the day when she realized she'd finally caught up to her mother in height. Now she was at least two inches taller. Sometimes this new perspective felt a little strange. She wondered how her mother felt about it. Or had it ever occurred to her?

"What were you and the boys so intent about?" Marti's mother asked.

"We were talking about Barry," Marti said. "And Thad." The sudden thought of Thad and what he might do terrified her so much that she shuddered.

For a moment her mother looked at her with concern. Then she pulled away and snapped off the living room light. As she joined Marti at the foot of the stairs she linked arms with her and said, "I know this is a difficult period for you, darling, but it will pass. It may seem like small consolation right now, but believe me, sweetheart, time will heal the pain."

"Yes, Mom," Marti murmured, but her mind was on Thad.

Her mother leaned on her as they climbed the stairs, and Marti could hear the catch in her breath. "I love you, Marti," her mother said. "You're a dear, good girl."

"I love you too, Mom," Marti answered. At the top of the stairs she parted from her mother with a quick kiss on the cheek, shut her bedroom door, and dialed the phone with trembling fingers.

It was answered in stereo, Charlie on one extension, a grumbling voice, soggy with sleep, on the other.

"Charlie?" Marti asked.

"Who is this? What time is it?" the deeper voice asked.

"I've got it, Dad," Charlie said quickly. "You can hang up."

His father muttered something, and Marti could hear the click as he put down the phone. She said, "It's Marti."

"I know it's you," Charlie said. "Listen, Marti, I'm not

going to explain this thing over the phone. I said tomorrow afternoon, and that's it."

"I'm calling about something else," Marti said. "I thought about it after you left. It's about Thad."

There was a pause before Charlie spoke, his voice thick with suspicion. "What about Thad?"

"Did Thad know where your gun was?"

"We all did."

"Then maybe Thad took it. Maybe Thad wanted to get even with the rest of you because you testified against him. Maybe Thad killed Barry. So—"

"You're just guessing. We don't know that."

"Charlie!" Marti gripped the receiver the way she'd have liked to grip Charlie's shoulders, forcing him to listen, to pay attention. Her breathing was ragged and shallow. It hurt to take a deep breath. "Listen to me! What I'm trying to say is, I want you to be very careful. Maybe it would be a good idea if you told the police what you've told me and what you're going to tell me tomorrow."

"The police?" Charlie burst out.

"Don't you see?" she said, and she was suddenly so overwhelmed with fear it was hard to speak. "If Thad's the one who killed Barry, then maybe he thinks he's got a reason to kill you and Tony too!"

CHAPTER · 10

It was hard to get through the day. Marti needed to talk to Karen and to hear what Charlie had to tell her. She was nervous when Charlie didn't show up for English lit class.

"He's sick," Tony said when the class was over. Even though the classroom was emptying as fast as a glass with a hole in the bottom, he kept his voice low.

She glanced to each side, but only a few people were in the room, and they were busy, not paying attention to Tony and Marti. Mr. Thompson was at the board explaining something to Carol Ann and Donna, and Emmet seemed to be sorting through the papers in his notebook. She figured that they were not even within earshot. "If Charlie's sick, I guess he won't want to meet with us," she said.

"We'll meet," Tony answered. "I think it would be better for Charlie to tell you what he has to say and get it off his chest. He's scared, that's all, and it's made him sick. He told me what you said when you called last night."

"I'm frightened for him—and for you too."

Tony shrugged. "So far, what do we know? It's all guesswork."

Marti frowned. "How can you possibly think that Barry killed himself?"

"I don't know what to think," Tony said, "but I'm not going to spend my life in the bathroom upchucking because I'm scared. I'll see you later at Charlie's house."

"As soon as I can make it," Marti said, but first there was the ordeal to get through in Miss Dillard's office. The counselor had sent her a reminder note, and Marti knew there was no getting out of the meeting. She just hoped she could keep it brief.

As Marti rushed from her locker, Kim grabbed at her arm, causing Marti to spin around. "Wait for me!" Kim shouted. "Where are you going so fast?"

"Miss Dillard's office," Marti said.

"I'll go with you."

Marti shook her head. "No," she said. "Miss Dillard wouldn't like it."

"Then let's get together afterward. Let's do something. Do you want to go to a movie tonight?"

"I thought you had a date."

Kim shrugged and looked a little sheepish. "It's not important. I can get out of it. I'd rather spend some time with you."

"You don't have to worry about me," Marti snapped. Seeing the hurt look on Kim's face, she leaned against the lockers and said, "Oh, Kim, I'm sorry. I didn't mean it like that."

112

"I know," Kim said. A smile wavered at the corners of her mouth and gave up. "Marti, you know that I—"

"Marti?" A voice interrupted.

Marti turned to see Karen Prescott. She was dressed in a faded denim skirt and a white blouse and, with her short, curly hair and freckled nose, looked like one of the students at Farrington Park High. "I was pretty sure I'd find you if I just looked around a bit," Karen said.

"Karen, this is my friend, Kim Roberts. Kim, this is Officer Karen Prescott."

"Officer?" Kim looked from Marti to Karen and back to Marti. "*Officer* Prescott?" she repeated.

"I'm on the staff of the Farrington Park Police Department," Karen said.

"Police?" It all seemed to come together for Kim. Her eyes opened a little wider and she said, "Oh. It's about Barry, isn't it? About Marti not being able to believe that Barry . . . that Barry—" She leaned forward intently. "Do you think Marti is right?"

"All we're doing is some preliminary informal investigating," Karen told her. "We haven't reached any conclusions yet. We may never be able to."

Marti got right to the point. "Why did you come here to find me?"

"I have some information for you," Karen said.

"What?" Marti asked in a rush. "Will it help us?"

"If you want me to stick around, I can," Kim said.

Marti shook her head. "I have to meet with the senior counselor," she said to Karen. "I almost forgot."

"I'll go with you," Karen told her.

"Wouldn't you like me to go too?" Kim asked. She moved a protective step closer to Marti.

"I'll call you tomorrow, Kim," Marti said. "We'll get

113

together." She looked at her watch. "I'd better get to Miss Dillard's office. It's getting late."

Marti walked down the nearly empty hall, Karen beside her. She hated the fact that she had left Kim looking like a puppy that had been left out in the rain, but Kim thought Marti was wrong. She wouldn't have helped. She'd have sat in Miss Dillard's office like a constant reminder that Marti couldn't accept the truth.

They rounded a corner to see Miss Dillard waiting in the hallway. The pucker between her eyebrows smoothed itself out as she saw Marti approach, but she glanced at Karen with curiosity.

"You're running a little late," Miss Dillard said to Marti. "Say good-bye to your friend, and come with me. I don't want to keep Dr. Granberry waiting any longer."

"Miss Dillard, this is Officer Karen Prescott. She's with the Farrington Park Police Department," Marti said.

Miss Dillard's eyebrows lifted. "Is this a joke? I mean, you look like one of our students."

Karen sighed. "I'm old enough to be a qualified police officer. I'll be glad to show you my identification."

After a pause Miss Dillard shook her head. "There's no need for that. I just hope that Marti told you she has an appointment with me."

"Yes," Karen said. "If you don't mind, I'd like to sit in. I won't interrupt. I'll try not to be in the way. I think it may be more helpful to me than hearing about the conversation later from Marti."

"Than hearing about—" Miss Dillard blinked rapidly and smoothed her skirt. "You're a police officer. I don't quite understand all this."

114

"Marti has asked me to help find the answers to some questions she has concerning Barry Logan's death."

"Oh, dear." Miss Dillard's glance was deep with sympathy as she looked at Marti before turning back to Karen. She seemed to fumble for the right words to say. "The medical examiner made a decision based on the facts. Marti is the only one who can't accept . . . Marti and Barry were close friends. Denial, up to a certain point, is normal, but surely, Miss—um—Prescott, you don't agree with Marti that Barry was murdered?" .

"I'm conducting an investigation. I have to keep an open mind," Karen answered.

Miss Dillard put an arm around Marti's shoulders and turned from the hall. "Very well. There's certainly no harm in having you present. Come with me. Dr. Granberry's waiting for us in my office."

Marti and Karen followed Miss Dillard through the reception office, down a short hallway, and into her own office. A tall man with a long nose and prominent teeth got up from one of the chairs next to Miss Dillard's desk and smiled easily. His deep blue suit hung well on his trim body, He adjusted his dark red silk tie and held out a hand. His smile was warm, and his voice was as smooth and polished as an actor's voice. By the time introductions had been made, Marti had the strange feeling that they were in *his* office, not Miss Dillard's.

As they seated themselves Dr. Granberry leaned forward, his eyes on Marti as though she were the most important person in the world. Marti pressed against the back of the chair, uncomfortable with his attention.

"I'm counting on your help, Marti," he said. "I'm trying an ambitious project, to be sure, but it's people like you who can help it succeed."

"I don't know how I can help you," Marti said.

He smiled brightly, leaned back, and didn't answer her question. "I'm sure you've seen that excellent television feature *Networking.*"

He paused, and Marti nodded.

She could hear the pride in his voice as he said, "They're sending Parker Grant here from New York to interview me—and some of the students—for a special that's already under way."

"Is the special about suicide?" Marti gripped the arms of her chair.

"Of course," Dr. Granberry said. "Our country has a growing problem of teen suicides. We need to discuss this publicly, to call attention to it. I'm sure you'll agree."

"I'll agree," Marti said, "as long as you leave Barry out of it."

"Miss Dillard told me that you're expressing a lot of denial regarding your friend's death," Dr. Granberry said.

"I'm not denying that Barry died. I know it happened, and it makes me sick. It hurts terribly every time I think about it. The only part I'm denying is that Barry took his own life."

Although Miss Dillard shot little sideways warning glances at Dr. Granberry, he seemed to ignore her. He leaned toward Marti and said, "Wake up, Marti. Face facts. Can't you see it's wishful thinking on your part?"

"Dr. Granberry," Miss Dillard said abruptly, "Marti's still feeling a great deal of shock and pain. I don't think your blunt approach is appropriate. You led me to believe that—"

Marti interrupted, shaking her head at Dr.

Granberry. "You're wrong about Barry, and I'm trying to prove it."

Dr. Granberry turned sharply toward Karen. "Are you helping her persist in her mistaken theory?"

"Dr. Granberry!" Miss Dillard said, but Karen answered him calmly.

"I'm a police officer. I investigate," Karen said. "I work with evidence, with facts, not with unfounded theories."

"You haven't even asked me why I know," Marti told Dr. Granberry.

He looked surprised, but folded his hands and quietly said, "Suppose you tell me."

"The gun was in his right hand, but Barry was left-handed."

"Interesting," he said, "but inconclusive."

"There was a bruise at the back of his head." When Dr. Granberry didn't respond, Marti added, "And we think that someone took some photographs from Barry's room." She stopped, resenting the broad smile that spread onto his face.

"I'm afraid you haven't convinced me," Dr. Granberry said. "I doubt if that story could convince anyone." He gave Karen a quick, impatient glance and turned back to Marti, his voice suave. "You don't really want to put a stumbling block in the way of my project, do you?"

"That's not what I'm trying to do," Marti said. "I just want to stop you from using Barry's death as an example of a teen suicide. Don't you want the truth?"

"We know what the truth is. And I've signed a high five-figure contract with my publisher, based on that truth." Dr. Granberry's voice slid from his throat like cream. "Marti, don't you see how many young people might be helped if we can show how the copycat syndrome exists, how it might be changed?"

"Is treating Barry's death as a copycat suicide the only way you can do this?"

"There've been other examples, but Barry's is the most current. Our data will be fresher with Barry's case."

Marti stood. "Your data will be wrong," she said. "I promise you that I'm going to prove it."

Miss Dillard got to her feet and reached out as Marti passed, resting her hand for an instant on Marti's arm. "I'm sorry, Marti," she said. "I didn't expect—"

"It's okay," Marti answered, but it wasn't. Her anger at Dr. Granberry burned inside her chest.

Their heels on the hard floors echoing like a loud tattoo, Karen followed Marti from the office, across the hall, and out the double doors of the main building. Once outside, Marti sighed and mumbled, "What is he trying to do?"

"I think that basically he's trying to do something worthwhile."

Marti turned to her, surprised. "You do?"

"Yes, and I think you're trying to do something worthwhile too."

"But we're both on different courses. It doesn't make sense."

"The truth makes sense, and that's what we're looking for," Karen said. She led the way down the steps. "I've got some information I can give you now. Remember, I told you I'd request a follow-up on the gun found at the scene? Okay. HPD came up with the name

118

of the person who bought and registered the gun. It's going to surprise you."

Marti put a hand on Karen's arm. "If you don't mind coming with me," she said, "I think there's someone you'd better talk to."

CHAPTER · 11

At first Charlie was resentful. He slumped on the sofa, legs sticking out into the room, and glared at Marti. "What I told you was confidential. I didn't know you were a snitch."

"I'm *not* a snitch!" Marti retorted.

But Karen put up a hand to stop her and said, "Your name was on the gun's registration, Charlie. Marti didn't have to tell me that. I came to her with the information."

Charlie squeezed his eyes tightly shut and groaned. "Why'd we do such a dumb thing?" he muttered.

"You can help yourself by being open with me," Karen said. "Tell me what you told Marti last night, along with what you planned to tell her today."

"I think you should," Tony said. He wedged himself next to Charlie as though he were giving his friend moral support.

Charlie, almost in a monotone, repeated what he had told Marti the night before.

When he'd finished, he looked defensively at Karen, as if he expected her criticism; but Karen—who had taken notes—simply looked up from her notepad and said, "Let's talk about Thad Miller's arrest and conviction for armed robbery. Was this Rossi .22 the gun he used?"

Tony's eyes bulged, and Charlie's mouth worked like a newly caught fish just pulled from the water. "H-how'd you know?" Charlie stammered.

"I thought Thad used a toy gun!" Marti whispered, but Karen ignored her.

"Did the other Cuatros take part in the robbery?" Karen asked.

"No!" Tony and Charlie shouted in unison.

Charlie added, "Thad liked to do crazy stuff. He was always coming up with wild ideas. He kept saying that since we had a gun, we ought to use it, that it would be exciting to see what would happen. At first we thought he was just kidding. Then he started talking about all of us wearing ski masks and robbing the jewelry store, and a lot of other stuff like that, but we wouldn't go along with it."

"Just like we said at the trial," Tony added. "We didn't really think Thad was going to do it, either. We thought he was all talk."

"I read the transcript," Karen said. "At the trial Thad claimed it was a kind of initiation stunt he had to go through. You two and Barry denied it."

"We denied it because Thad was lying," Charlie said. "We weren't a gang. We didn't want to rob anybody. We told him that the robbery was a stupid idea."

"That's the truth. I hope you believe us," Tony said.

"How did Thad react when the three of you testified against him?"

"Just what you'd think. He didn't like it much. Neither did his family." Tony hunched his shoulders, adding, "I remember the way they kept staring at us all through the trial."

"Did Thad make any threats against any of you?"

"No."

"Was he more angry at Barry than at either of you?"

Tony and Charlie glanced at each other. Charlie looked sick again. "I don't think so," he mumbled.

Karen stared into Charlie's eyes as though she could see beyond them into his cache of secrets. "Were you aware that Thad planned to use the .22 in the robbery?"

"No," Charlie said.

"When were you aware he had taken the gun?"

"None of this came up in the trial." Charlie squirmed even lower on the sofa.

"It doesn't matter. And please don't think you're on trial right now. We're just trying to sort out the facts and see what they add up to. Okay?"

Charlie was silent, and Marti could see his Adam's apple working. She tried to help him out. "At the trial," she said, "Thad insisted it was a toy gun, and he said he'd thrown it into the bayou."

"I've read the transcript," Karen repeated.

"Oh, I—I f-forgot," Marti stammered. She sank back against the cushions on the sofa, both impressed and intimidated by Karen's professional manner. When Karen was easygoing and friendly, Marti began to think of her as a friend. But now she was all business, a person very different from the smiling woman who liked diet colas. Could one of the Karens ever get lost inside the other and never come out again? Is this what it was like to be a cop?

"Charlie," Karen said in a no-nonsense voice, "suppose you answer my question now. When were you aware that Thad had taken the gun?"

"A few days after the robbery," Charlie said, "when Thad brought it back." He clapped the palms of his hands over his forehead and squeezed his eyes shut again. The others waited until he was able to continue.

"Thad was scared," Charlie said. "According to Thad, the owner of the place where he'd stolen the jewelry kept staring at the gun, so Thad decided to get rid of it. He planned to throw it in the bayou, but he was afraid it might be recovered. He didn't want that to happen. If no one could produce a gun, Thad figured it would come down to just his word against the shop owner's, and he'd be better off."

"Which he probably was," Karen said. "Go on, Charlie. What arrangement did you make with Thad?"

Charlie put his hands down and looked at her through narrowed eyes.

"I'm not reading your mind," she said. "I'm adding up facts to get answers. Please tell me. What arrangement did you make?"

"I was the only one of the Cuatros who knew that Thad had used the gun," Charlie said. "Barry and Tony were suspicious at first, after Thad was arrested, because Thad had wanted to use our .22, but when he kept insisting he'd used a toy gun, and I showed them the .22 still in the hiding place, they believed him." He gulped hard and added, "I never told anyone what had happened—not until I saw that picture in the newspaper, when they wrote the story about Barry and found out that our gun was missing. Then I told Tony."

124

Charlie squirmed upward and scowled. "Hey, look! If they'd asked me about it at the trial, I might have said something, but no one but the Cuatros knew that we had that gun, so no one asked about it. I wasn't lying under oath. Nobody asked!"

"You don't have to defend yourself," Karen said.

"Well, the way you're looking at me, you make me feel—" He didn't finish the sentence.

Marti broke in. "Why were you trying to protect Thad by not telling the truth about the gun? By trying to keep those photographs away from me so I wouldn't see the gun?"

Charlie exploded, "We weren't trying to protect Thad! We were trying to protect *ourselves*! *I'm* the one whose name is on the registration. If that had come out at the trial, *all* the Cuatros would have looked guilty. And if everyone knew that the gun that killed Barry was mine—" He leaned back and let out a groan.

"When they found the gun with Barry," Marti asked, "why didn't they check the registration?"

"Since there was no evidence of foul play, there was no need to," Karen answered. She waited a minute, then asked, "Is there anything else you want to tell us, Charlie?"

"That's it," he said. "I told you everything."

Karen turned her gaze on Tony. "How about you, Tony? Can you think of anything else?"

Tony shrugged and shook his head.

"Marti?"

"I have another question," Marti said. "Charlie, you didn't know that Thad had taken the gun."

"That's what I already said. Weren't you listening?"

"I'm not finished," Marti complained. "What I'm getting at is this: Did Thad get into your house while you

125

and your parents weren't there, in order to get the gun? Or did someone let him in?"

"Nobody let him in. He told me he'd let himself in and taken the gun."

"Aren't you and your parents in the habit of locking your doors?" Karen asked.

"Sure we lock the doors," Charlie said. His eyes widened. "Oh. I see what you mean."

Karen got up and left the room. They could hear her footsteps in the entry hall. When she returned she said, "No dead bolts. The kind of locks builders put in outside doors can be opened in two seconds by someone who knows what he's doing."

"We hardly ever have a burglary around here," Tony said. "Nobody thinks about stuff like dead bolts."

"I think we've covered everything for now," Karen said. She gave her business cards to Tony and Charlie. "I appreciate your cooperation."

"Am I going to get into trouble about keeping the gun for Thad?" Charlie asked as he stood to join the others. His shirt was wet with sweat.

"No," Karen said.

"Do you think Thad could have come back?"

"I don't know," she answered. "I traced his whereabouts, and I've talked to members of his family in the Austin area. They've given him a strong alibi."

"So it wasn't Thad," Marti murmured.

"I didn't say that," Karen said. "Family members have been known to lie to protect one another."

"It's a strange family," Tony said.

"What do you mean?" Karen asked him.

"Well, I just mean that Thad was always full of wild ideas. He'd even do really dangerous stunts, like he didn't care what happened to him. Emmet—he's the

brightest one, and his parents claim he's a genius—
Emmet's so quiet and strange, he hardly ever talks to
anybody. Sometimes when I was over at Thad's house,
I'd start to feel uncomfortable and find Emmet had
sneaked into the room and was staring at me. He could
always make me feel creepy. And Thad's parents are
. . . well, they're not friendly. They're always kind of
formal and cold."

Charlie nodded. "They might lie for Thad. All of
them."

Karen walked to the door, and they followed her. She
ran one finger down the doorframe. "Tell your parents
it would be a good idea to get dead bolts installed on
your doors," she said. "Tell them it's recommended by
the Farrington Park Police Department."

Charlie frowned as he said to Karen, "I don't like all
this—all that you're doing. The police said that Barry
committed suicide. So did the coroner. As far as I'm
concerned, Barry's the one who took the gun from my
house. He knew where it was. He could have. You
haven't got any proof that he didn't kill himself, have
you? All the proof seems to be that he did."

Marti spoke up. "Proof? How can you ask about—"

"Shut up, Marti," he said. "If you keep on with what
you're doing, other people might start asking the same
questions about the robbery and the gun that your cop
friend just came up with. You'll end up getting Tony
and me into trouble."

Marti had her mouth open to answer, when Karen
put a restraining hand on her arm. "You're right about a
lack of court-admissible evidence," Karen said to Charlie. "But Marti had some legitimate questions, and
we're looking for the answers."

127

"You can't bring Barry back. Why don't you just let it alone?"

"If we can't come up with answers within a reasonable length of time, we'll have to," Karen said. She beckoned to Marti. "Come on. I'll give you a ride home."

Marti ran to catch up with Karen as she strode down the walk. "I can walk home," she said. "I live just around the corner on the next block."

"I'd like to check your house too," Karen said.

"I can give you the answer right now," Marti answered. "No dead bolts." She looked puzzled. "I could tell that you want extra protection for Charlie and Tony, but why do you think my family would need them?"

Karen glanced at her sharply, then said, "Everybody needs them. Crimes take place in small towns as well as in large cities."

As she opened the door on the passenger side of the car, Marti said, "Karen, what you told Charlie about your investigation—there's more, isn't there? I mean, you agree with me that Barry was murdered, don't you?"

"As I said, there are questions that need answers." She paused. "Marti, I don't like the loose ends in this situation. I'm inclined to think that you may be right."

With a sense of relief, Marti settled on the front seat of the small sedan and watched Karen turn on the ignition and drive away from the curb. "You're not on duty? No uniform, no cop car."

Karen smiled. "Free time right now. I'm subbing for another officer and taking his shift later tonight."

Marti looked at her curiously. "Who answered your phone last night? He has a nice voice."

128

"Yes, he does. He's a nice person."

"Your boyfriend?"

"My former partner at HPD."

"Why did you leave the Houston Police Department?"

Karen shrugged. "I guess I wanted to try life in the slow lane."

"Was there that much crime? Were you afraid of being killed?"

"You're dramatizing it, Marti. Being a police officer is a job, and it's a job I like. Afraid? No. Alert? Yes."

"When you said the slow lane, did that mean you wanted to get away from your partner?"

For an instant Karen twisted to look at her sharply. "This is pretty far off the subject, isn't it?"

"I've been watching you," Marti said. "Sometimes you're all business, but sometimes you relax and you're a . . . well, a regular person. I was kind of hoping that now you'd want to be a person again."

"A person or a cop." Karen was silent for a few moments, then turned to Marti with a shrug and an attempted smile. "Okay. I'll try to be a person for a while."

"I didn't mean to be rude," Marti said.

"You weren't. In your own way you gave me the same kind of message I've been getting from someone else."

"Your former partner?"

Karen smiled again and raised one eyebrow. "What's all this interest in my partner?"

"I haven't got a right to pry," Marti said. "I just sort of wondered if you and your partner were like Barry and me."

"You said you weren't in love with Barry." Karen

suddenly made a funny sound in the back of her throat, and her cheeks grew pink.

Marti looked away, trying to help Karen cover her embarrassment. "I think maybe I *was* in love with Barry," she said. "I trusted him. I believed in him. I was happy when I was with him. Is that what love is?"

Karen was silent for a moment before she answered. "I suppose."

As they came around the curve on Castle Lake Drive, Marti suddenly spotted a light gray car ahead of them. It wasn't parked. It was moving, and it turned off onto the next street.

"What's the matter?" Karen asked her, and Marti realized that she was sitting upright, clutching the door handle.

"It was that car," she said. "The gray car. A few days ago I thought that someone in a car like that followed me home. Then I saw a light gray car parked down the street from the church when I went to talk to Dr. Emery."

"Did it follow you?"

"No. I went out the back door to the street behind the church."

"Was it the same car?"

"I don't know."

"Did you see who was in the car on either occasion?"

Karen parked in front of Marti's house, and Marti leaned back against the seat. She opened the door on her side of the car. "No," she said.

"There are lots of light gray cars," Karen told her. "However, I'll check out your house, just to make sure everything is all right."

Marti unlocked the front door and waited in the entry hall while Karen went through all the rooms. "Everything looks all right," she said when she returned in a few minutes. "All the doors and windows are locked."

"Since this is your dinnertime, would you like something to eat?" Marti asked. "I'm making frozen dinners tonight, and I can put one in the microwave for you right now. It will take just a couple of minutes."

"Well . . ." Karen hesitated.

"Come back to the kitchen with me," Marti told her. "Do you like braised beef tips in red wine sauce?"

"Sounds great."

Marti dropped her books on the table, washed her hands, and pulled one of the frozen dinner packages out of the freezer. "Sit down," she said, waving a hand toward the chairs at the kitchen table. "Iced tea okay to drink? We've got lots of milk too."

"Iced tea will be fine," Karen said.

Within a few minutes Marti served Karen a steaming hot dinner, an iceberg lettuce-and-tomato salad, and a glass of tea.

"Do you like to cook?" Karen asked as she dug into the salad.

"I don't mind it. But I don't want to talk about cooking. Let's finish the conversation we were having."

Karen looked up, surprised. "About what?"

"About men. About being in love."

Karen smiled, but she shook her head. "I'm the wrong one to ask. Police officers should never fall in love." Karen ate quickly, as though she were unused to enjoying a meal in leisure.

"Why not?"

"For one thing, the hours are terrible. When you're on a case you're away from your family, sometimes for days at a time. You live with a case; you sleep with it; you're with your partner more than you're with your

131

husband or wife. It's too tough on a marriage." She paused. "I'd guess that no other profession causes more broken marriages."

"Maybe it's not the fault of the police officers. Maybe it's the fault of the people they marry," Marti said.

Karen patted at her lips with her napkin. "Why do you say that?"

Marti shrugged. "Because a big part of love is trust, isn't it?"

Karen blinked a couple of times, and her cheeks grew pink again. She pushed back her chair and got to her feet. "Thanks for the dinner," she said. "I'd better report for duty."

Marti walked with her to the door. She felt comfortable with Karen now. She liked her. "Any time," she said. "I don't usually make microwave dinners."

Karen tapped at the edge of the open door. "Dead bolts," she said. She smiled and ran down the walk to her car.

Marti went back to the kitchen and flipped on the television set before she put the dishes Karen had used into the dishwasher. She turned to one of the independent stations. They'd be showing an old situation comedy, something that could be watched without thinking.

"News brief on the hour," the announcer was saying. "Attorneys for the rock group Flesh deny that 'Sudden Death,' their popular recording, encourages teen suicide, specifically the triple suicides of teenagers from the Houston area, and vow to fight the church and civic groups that are organizing across the country to demand censorship of music deemed harmful to young people.

"Taking the opposing side, Dr. Jerome Emery claims

he was inspired to lead his crusade against Flesh and other hard-rock and heavy-metal groups because he feels they were strongly involved in the tragic suicide of a young member of his congregation. Tonight, following the ten o'clock news, we'll host a panel discussion with Dr. Emery and visiting psychologist and best-selling author, Dr. Clement Granberry.

"Today in Moscow . . ."

Marti snapped off the set, held her head in her hands, and shouted, "No, no, no! You're not being fair to Barry!" She leaned against the refrigerator and tried to think. What could she do? She had tried to explain about Barry to Dr. Emery, but he was like all the other adults. He thought she didn't know what she was talking about.

There was only one thing that could change his mind. With Karen's help, she'd have to keep trying to find Barry's murderer. It was the only way she could prove that Barry didn't take his own life.

Marti slowly walked upstairs and into her room. She stood at the window, looking across to the tightly closed blinds in Barry's bedroom window. She tried to remember the room as it had been when Barry had been alive, but all she could see in her mind was the horror of the room as it had been torn apart.

"Oh, Barry," she whispered as a tear rolled down her cheek. "I miss you so much."

Marti turned, rubbing at her eyes, and headed for her bed. She was tired—so terribly tired. Maybe, if she rested for just a few minutes . . .

As she reached the bed she stopped short. She clutched her throat, choking off a strangled scream. On her pillow lay Barry's baseball cap.

CHAPTER · 12

Someone had been in the house. He'd come to her room and laid the cap on her bed. The murderer. It couldn't be anyone else.

Marti's skin crawled as she felt the hatred that lingered behind him like slime from a snail. She could smell his sweat, his anger, the sickness that oozed from his fingertips as he touched Barry's cap and her bed.

Furious, she snatched up the cap, clutching it to her chest with one hand while, with the other, she ripped the spread from her bed and threw it to the floor. Someone had dared to touch something private and special that had belonged to Barry. He had dared to violate her bedroom.

Shuddering with disgust Marti huddled on the floor, her cheek against Barry's cap, and wailed loudly, as a child would cry, until there were no more tears and dry, hiccuping sobs shook her body. She sat up and stroked the stained, battered cap, more determined than ever to discover the identity of the person who had killed Barry.

"Thad," she said through clenched teeth, "was it you?"

By the time her parents arrived home, Marti was in command of herself. She'd made a big salad of mixed greens and arranged a small platter of thin breadsticks and toast thins, so that preparing dinner was simply a matter of heating the frozen dinners in the microwave.

Both her mother and father had office conversation to relate, but finally there was a moment of silence and Marti told her parents that the Farrington Park Police Department was recommending that dead bolts be installed on the doors.

"That's odd," her mother said. "I've never felt the need for dead bolts. They seem to go with city problems, which is one reason we left Houston."

"It's important," Marti insisted.

"We'll certainly think about it," her father reassured her. "It's no problem to have them installed."

Marti's mother put down her fork, leaned back in her chair, and sighed happily. "I love Friday evenings," she said. "No pressures, no alarm clock to set for tomorrow morning." She looked toward her husband. "Why don't we do something tonight, Josh? Want to go to a movie?"

"I don't know," her father said. "What's at the Six?"

"A new Bruce Willis film," she said. "It got good reviews in the *Houston Chronicle*. It's supposed to be very funny." She turned to Marti. "Are you and Kim going anywhere tonight?"

"Kim's got a date," Marti said.

Her mother's face brightened. "Then you can come with us," she said. "How wonderful! For a change we'll do something together as a family. You're usually off and away with your own projects." She reached across the table and took Marti's hand. "Please come, Marti."

Her father, who'd been thumbing through the newspaper, looked up and said, "The next show goes on in thirty minutes. We can make it."

"Marti?" her mother asked.

"I'm not very good company," Marti said.

"You are to us."

Her parents waited for her answer, looking at her with such an eager intentness that Marti nodded. "Okay," she said. "I'll go with you."

The movie was funny, she supposed. Now and then the audience laughed, and her parents looked pleased as the lights came on and the audience began straggling out. Marti hadn't been able to keep her mind on the plot. If anyone had asked what the story was about, she wouldn't have been able to tell them.

"That was fun," Marti's mother said. "Wasn't that fun?"

"Who wants ice cream?" her father asked.

Marti felt as though she'd been carried back in time, as though she were ten years old. A movie, with popcorn, and ice cream afterward. Is this what her parents did whenever they went out to a movie together? Was it a pattern that never changed? What about their jobs, their evenings? One day following another. Was each of them the same? The ice cream, fragrant with crushed strawberries, numbed her tongue. She glanced toward her mother and father, studying them from under her lashes. They were different, older. It was almost as though they were strangers. She wondered what they really wanted to do with their lives, what wishes and yearnings they had, what they thought about.

"Are you having a good time, darling?" her mother asked.

"Sure," Marti said.

Half an hour later, as they walked into the house, Marti looked at her watch. Ten-twenty.

"That new comic I like—I forget his name, but you know who I mean—is going to be a guest on the talk show tonight," her father said. "He's good. Why don't we watch him?"

Marti eyed her books, which she'd moved to one of the kitchen counters. "I think I'll catch up on some homework," she said. "I'll just work here at the kitchen table."

"If you want anything," her mother said, "we'll be in the den."

Marti smiled. Her mother was trying to help her. It wasn't her fault that they couldn't seem to say the right things to each other. As her parents left the room Marti spread her books on the kitchen table, opening her textbook to the chapter assigned in history. Then she reached for the remote control, turning on the television, which was still set to the independent channel.

For a few moments she actually read a few pages, but when the panel show began and the guests were announced, she closed the book and gave her full attention to the program.

Dillis Jansen, the well-dressed, dark-haired woman who hosted so many of the channel's locally produced programs, leaned forward in her upholstered chair and graciously introduced her two guests, who were seated on a sofa next to her. "And of course, Farrington Park is such a near neighbor that we consider it almost a part of Houston," Dillis said.

She turned from her guests to the camera. "After the interview with our two special guests, who were so kind and so concerned about this problem of teen suicide that they agreed on very short notice to appear on our program, we'll open the program to you—the audience —for telephone calls. The number will appear on your screen. Remember, if you have any questions to ask either of these two gentlemen, or if you have any information or personal experiences you want to add, jot down the number and give us a call."

Dillis Jansen gave a little wiggle of her shoulders as she settled into her job of interviewing. "I'd like to ask you first, Dr. Granberry—and may I add that your latest book on family relationships is simply marvelous—why do—?"

"*Actions and Reactions.* Have to get that title in." He chuckled.

"Of course. And I heartily recommend your book to everyone. Truly marvelous." Dillis didn't miss a beat and went right into her question. "Why do you think so many teenagers choose to commit suicide?"

Dr. Granberry shook his head. "There are a number of reasons. They find themselves in situations they can't cope with. Sometimes it's parental rejection or divorce. Sometimes it's pressures and demands from their peers or from parents and teachers. Sometimes it's an attempt to punish someone close to them. In all cases, it boils down to a total loss of hope. Suicide becomes a cry for help."

"A cry for help? Then how can they feel that killing themselves is the answer?"

"Studies have shown that many teenagers are unable

to fully comprehend the fact that death is final. To them suicide is an act of desperation in which they are crying out, 'Listen to me! Help me!' without realizing they will have removed themselves from any help that could be given."

"But don't they ask for this help ahead of time? Aren't there signs that parents could look for?"

"Oh, yes," he said. "Symptoms of depression, social or school problems, inability to sleep, talking about suicide, giving away possessions—some potential suicide victims show very definite signs."

"Don't they ever just talk to a parent? Don't they say, 'This is how I feel'?"

"If the family members are close, if children have parents who listen and try to help, they'll usually talk." He shifted a little, as though the sofa were lumpy, and added, "However, today the close, intimate two-parent undivided family is becoming a rarity."

Dillis's forehead puckered. "Why do these young people give up hope? Don't they know that each of them is a very special individual with the ability to rise above his or her problems? Lots of people have had terrible problems and have been able to solve them. Is it a matter of not knowing whom to turn to? Not knowing how?"

"That enters into it," Dr. Granberry said. "Besides problems within the family, many teenagers today have serious problems in their relationships with each other. For example, early sexual involvement, with a subsequent break-up of the relationship, often causes pain these kids don't know how to handle."

"Like the two students in our area who committed suicide last May."

"Exactly, and unfortunately around our nation we

140

are experiencing what is called the copycat syndrome, meaning that a young person who is depressed commits suicide because others have. This could very well be the case with the promising student in Farrington Park who ended his life last week."

Marti clutched the edge of the table and moaned. Nothing she had told him about Barry had made any difference. Nothing.

Dr. Emery suddenly leaned forward, injecting himself into the conversation. "I think that Dr. Granberry is ignoring something we must be well aware of, which is that many of the problems that lead to suicide are self-induced. Many young people who have committed suicide have been habitual drug or alcohol abusers. And some of the music they listen to—it *has* to be a dangerous influence."

"Dr. Emery, I was just about to ask you to tell us about your crusade against some of the hard-rock and heavy-metal groups," Dillis said smoothly. She looked into the camera. "Dr. Emery and I have been friends for years. In fact, he was my own minister before he was stolen away by Farrington Park, and I'm so in awe of the total devotion he's giving to his crusade."

"The lyrics to some of the popular songs contain words and ideas of explicit sex—even sexual violence—of horror, of despair," Dr. Emery said. "Again, the lyrics cause a terrible feeling of hopelessness." The song 'Sudden Death' by the group called Flesh is a definite invitation to suicide. Parents who haven't listened to the words of the latest popular songs can't imagine how horrible many of them are and what an evil influence they can have on their children."

In his intensity, Dr. Emery ran his hands through his white hair. A cowlick sprang up at the back of his head,

141

and a thick lock of hair fell over one eye. He cleared his throat and added, "Barry Logan is an example of what that kind of music can do to destroy a fine young mind and end a promising young life."

"Surely you aren't suggesting out-and-out censorship?" Dr. Granberry asked, and the television conversation shifted.

Marti rested her head on her arms and closed her eyes. Both these men had strong points they wanted to make, and both of them were using Barry as an example. A copycat suicide? Under the influence of Flesh? Not Barry. How could she make them listen to reason?

She sat up, turning her attention again to the program after she realized that a boy was now speaking on the station's telephone hook-up: ". . . but, like, most of the time, you know, you can't talk to your parents."

"Don't you think your father could find a few minutes to spend with you so you could talk things over?" Dr. Emery asked.

The telephone caller answered, "My Dad lives in Oregon with his second family. I haven't seen him for over a year."

Dillis leaned forward, as though the boy were in the room. "What about your mother? Do you live with your mother?"

"Yeah, but she's usually at work, you know, or out somewhere with the guy she's dating."

"Talk to your school counselor," Dr. Granberry said.

"Or to your minister," Dr. Emery quickly added. "Talk to someone."

"I'm going to give you a number. We'll put it on the screen right above our call-in number," Dillis said. On the screen appeared *(713) 228-1505.* "It's the number of the Houston Crisis Hotline. Someone's there twenty-four hours a day, so write it down and use it if you need it. If you need them now, call them. Someone will help you."

"I'm okay," the boy said. "I just, you know, wanted to say something about, you know, talking to parents."

"Thank you for calling," Dillis said. There was an audible click and she shifted position, asking Dr. Granberry, "How about Barry Logan? Do you know if he tried to talk to anyone about his problems?"

"Apparently not," Dr. Granberry said. Dr. Emery added, "His parents are concerned that Barry may have exhibited signs of depression, and they didn't pick up on them."

Dillis Jansen apparently received a signal, because she said, "We have another caller now. Hello? You're on the air."

A woman said, "I want to ask Dr. Emery if he's seen that musician, Ozzy . . . uh . . . whoever. I forget his name, the one who did that song "Suicide Solution" and has that picture of the gun pointing at his head? I mean that's just what Dr. Emery's talking about, and the minute I laid eyes on it, I took it away from my daughter, and—"

With shaking fingers Marti copied the call-in telephone number from the screen, walked to the kitchen phone, and dialed it. The voice that answered took her name, told her there were only two callers ahead of her, and asked her to be sure to turn down the sound on her set as soon as her call was put through. Marti turned the sound low immediately and leaned against the counter, where she could see the television set. The telephone receiver was damp in her clammy hands, and her stomach hurt.

They were on another call now, discussing warning

signs with the man who'd phoned in. Marti cleared her throat a couple of times. She wondered if she would be able to talk when her turn came. She was tempted to hang up.

"So we agree," Dillis said, "it's up to parents, counselors, clergy—responsible adults who can recognize signs in troubled teenagers."

The click came and Dillis said, "Hello? Hello?" After a pause she said, "That caller changed his mind. We'll take the next in line." Marti jumped as she heard in her ear "Hello? It's your turn. Do you have a question?"

"Yes," Marti said. "That is, it's not a question. It's just something I want to say." Her voice was rough, so she cleared her throat and began again. "I don't agree with some of the things that were said, like responsible adults looking for warning signs."

She could see the three people on television sitting at attention, waiting for her to continue. Dr. Emery's head was cocked and he looked a little puzzled, as though he were trying to place her voice. Marti took a deep breath and went on. "I know the warning signs are important, and I think everybody needs to know them to look for them—especially kids," she said. "Kids are more likely to talk about their problems with their friends. A lot of the parents I know are busy all the time. I guess they worry about their children, but they don't talk to them much. About important things, I mean. Kids are the ones who really know one another and know if a friend is having real problems."

She paused and Dillis Jansen said, "That's an interesting point. Our caller is saying that the responsibility of looking for warning signs should be taken by the teenagers themselves. Would either of you gentlemen like to comment on this?"

"Wait!" Marti said. "I'm not through. That was just the first part. The rest is that Barry Logan was my friend. If Barry had thought about committing suicide, *I* would have known it. And he hadn't. He was happy. He'd just been accepted by A & M, and he was planning for the future. He didn't kill himself!"

She realized her voice had risen, so she tried to lower it to a conversational tone. "Dr. Emery and Dr. Granberry—I don't think you realize what you're doing. You're both trying to do something helpful, but you're using Barry's death for your own purposes, so you don't want to recognize that he didn't kill himself. He—"

Dillis Jansen had turned to the others and was talking. Marti had been cut off.

Aching with frustration, Marti hung up the phone and raised the sound of the television set to a normal tone. Didn't they realize how hard it had been to make the call? Didn't they want to hear the truth?

Dr. Emery looked distressed and was running his fingers through his hair again, but Dr. Granberry had what could pass for a sympathetic smile on his face. ". . . the denial phase," he was saying. "To a point it can be considered normal. Her school counselor is aware of her problem."

Muttering under her breath, Marti jabbed the Off button on the television set.

The phone rang, and she answered it. "Nice going, Marti," the voice whispered.

145

CHAPTER • 13

"Who are you?" Marti demanded, but the person who had made the call had hung up.

Same voice. Same person who had called when she'd been listening to Dr. Emery once before.

Marti slammed down the phone, angry and embarrassed. Anyone who knew the strength of her feelings would have had no trouble guessing her identity after what she had said on the call-in show. Dillis Jansen had cut her off, and Dr. Granberry had attributed her statements to "problems." And now this creep had put its two cents in!

"Marti?" her mother said from the doorway. "Aren't you about ready to come to bed? I know that tomorrow's Saturday, but you've had a long, busy day."

"Okay," Marti answered. Hurt and discouraged, she slammed her books together, snatched them up, and followed her parents up the stairs and to bed.

She lay in the dark for a long time, unable to sleep, thinking of Barry, remembering the sound of his voice, of his laughter. She could still hear him below her bedroom window, calling out, Hey, Marti! Get up! Come on out!

Marti gasped, tensing, waiting, holding her breath. The voice seemed so real! Barry? In the silent dark she realized that the voice had been only inside her mind, a remnant of memory that had managed to escape. She burrowed into her pillow, trying to smother the pain, to think of something else. *How will I ever be able to sleep?* she wondered.

When the telephone woke her and she fumbled for it, Marti was surprised to find herself squinting into bright sunlight. She mumbled something, and heard Karen say, "I'm sorry. I woke you, didn't I? I thought you'd be up by now."

Marti struggled to a sitting position. "What time is it?"

"Close to ten. Want to go back to sleep, or do you want to hear the results I got from Latent Prints?"

"I want to hear," Marti said. "What's Latent Prints?"

"The department that works to identify fingerprints, in this case the ones we took in Barry's room—specifically on his photo album."

Marti was wide awake by this time. "Go on."

"We got some good, clear prints, but nothing we can go forward on at this point. Some of the prints are Barry's; one thumbprint was his father's. But there are others that were either too smeared to be any good or were made by people who had never had their fingerprints taken. Probably his mother's prints. Maybe a friend's."

"Or maybe the murderer's!" Marti paused. "Why

could they identify Barry's father's prints on the album, and not his mother's?"

"Because his father had probably served in one of the armed forces at some time in his life and had been fingerprinted, so those prints would be on file. There may have been no reason at any time for his mother to have been fingerprinted."

"How about Thad?" Marti asked.

"Thad would have been fingerprinted."

"Were his prints on the album?"

"None that we could find. But that's not conclusive. Remember, I told you there were a few prints that had been smeared."

"So Thad could have held the album."

"We have no proof one way or the other."

"Proof! Everybody keeps talking about proof!"

"That's what it takes to make a case," Karen said. "You know that."

"Yes, I do. I just wish this were easier to work out." Marti sighed. "So the fingerprints you got aren't any help at all."

"They could be," Karen said, "if we had a suspect and his prints matched those on the album."

"But not if the suspect is Thad."

"Speaking of Thad," Karen said, "his relatives weren't the only ones who confirmed his alibi. He also met with his probation officer in Austin, so it looks as though he's in the clear."

Marti drew her knees up under the blanket and rested her chin on them while she thought. "How long would it take to drive from Austin to Farrington Park?"

"Roughly three hours. Maybe a little less. Why?"

"He could have sneaked out when his family thought he was asleep. He wouldn't have been under their

149

noses every minute. And Thad's probation officer wouldn't have known he was out of town, either."

There was silence for a moment, until Karen said, "That's a pretty farfetched idea, Marti."

"But it's a possibility, isn't it? Think about it!"

"I'll let you get back to sleep," Karen said. "I'm going to be off until Monday. I'll check back with you then."

"Okay."

"Try to relax. Have a good weekend."

"You too." Marti paused. "What's his name?"

"Who?"

"Your former partner. You're going to see him, aren't you?"

"Yes, I am. His name is Greg Quinn. Satisfied?" Marti opened her mouth to ask another question, but Karen was too quick. "You'd better be," she said, a smile in her voice, "because that's all the information you're going to get."

"For now," Marti said.

Karen laughed. "I'll talk to you Monday."

Saturday was relatively quiet. Kim came over, and they did their nails and talked about Kim's Friday-night date, which had turned out to be a disaster. Before long, Marti found herself laughing and gossiping and giggling as though she had left an older, more tired shell of herself curled in a corner; and it wasn't until Kim went home that evening that Marti slipped back into her harder skin, wrapping it snugly around herself, allowing pain to seal up all the cracks.

On Sunday, Dr. Emery—after a sympathetic glance at Marti—explained to his congregation about the work that would demand every minute of his spare time— the tremendous task of trying to alert adults to the explicitness of violence and sex in much of the rock music their children were listening to—and he earnestly begged for the assistance of each and every member of his congregation. After the service, people crowded around him, shocked by some of the statistics and examples he had given them, and eager to help by signing either a petition or a check.

But Dr. Emery managed to work his way through to Marti, and he took her hand, his eyes searching hers. "How are you, Marti?" he asked.

"I'm fine now," Marti answered calmly, her thoughts of Barry a buffer between Dr. Emery and herself.

"You do understand now what I'm trying to do?" he asked.

Marti wanted to answer, I understood all along. It's you who can't understand me. But she simply nodded, thankful when her parents inserted themselves into the conversation by praising Dr. Emery for the stand he was taking.

It was Sunday afternoon when a rich, deep voice on the telephone identified himself to Marti as Parker Grant, top anchorman on the weekly national TV news magazine *Networking*. "I'm sure you've seen the program?" he asked with such arrogant certainty that Marti was tempted to fib and tell him that she never watched it.

But she answered politely and truthfully that her parents rarely missed his program. She was so familiar with his face that she could almost imagine his look of satisfaction.

"I'm planning a segment of my program to deal with the alarming rise in the number of teenage suicides, and I'll be filming in Farrington Park," he said. "I've received the cooperation of your school-district administrators, and I'll be interviewing both Dr. Clement Granberry and Dr. Jerome Emery, who are taking divergent but interesting views on how to handle the problem."

Marti didn't answer.

After a long pause he asked, "Marti? Are you still there?"

"Yes," she said. "But I don't understand why you called me."

"I was listening to the local program produced by a Houston independent channel on Friday night. I talked about it later with Granberry, and he identified you as the caller who couldn't accept her friend's suicide. I'd like to talk to you. I'd like to interview you on tape and film."

"Why?"

"Because you have a strong point of view. Right or wrong, your opinion would add a new dimension."

Hope was like an explosion in her chest. For an instant it was hard to take a breath, and she felt a little dizzy. Carefully, Marti sought the right words. "Sometimes on your program your reporters investigate situations you think are wrong," she said. "You say that you probe for the truth. Like when you exposed all the graft in that town in the Midwest."

"That's right."

"Well, then, is that what you plan to do? Will you try to find the proof that Barry was murdered?"

He cleared his throat, then said, "That wouldn't fit into the parameters on this one, Marti. We've mapped our direction, and we plan to deal with the background of suicide and what can be done to prevent it. Looking into an allegation of murder would be a side issue. It would detract from the whole picture. Do you see what I mean?"

"Yes," Marti said, her throat so tight that it hurt.

"So suppose we make an appointment for an interview? What's a good time for you?"

"Never," Marti said. "I'm outside your parameters too." She hung up the telephone.

He called an hour later and talked to her mother. "Marti," she said when she found her in the kitchen, munching on an apple, "you'll never guess who is on the phone! Parker Grant! I'm so excited! We were actually having a conversation, and he sounds like such a nice person."

She started, as though she had suddenly remembered his message. "He wants to interview you for national television. He wanted me to make the appointment, but I said I'd leave it up to you."

"Did he tell you why he wants to interview me?" Marti asked.

"Just that they're going to do a program about teen suicides. Mr. Grant seems terribly concerned and hopes his program will help reduce the problem. Those were his exact words. He thinks you could talk about Barry, since the two of you were such close friends."

Marti hated to erase the excitement on her mother's face, but she said, "Mom, on Friday night I was watching a TV interview show with Dillis Jansen and Dr. Emery and Dr. Granberry. They had a call-in period, so I called them and complained that both Dr. Emery and Dr. Granberry were using Barry to suit their own purposes."

"Oh, dear! You said this to Dr. Emery?"

"I'm sorry if I embarrassed you, Mom, but it was something I had to do. They can't keep talking about how Barry killed himself, when he didn't! I know he didn't!"

Her mother's cheeks seemed to sag and she looked more tired than she sometimes did on a day when she'd had an especially heavy work load at the office. "Then I don't understand why Mr. Grant called you," she murmured.

"Because I'm supposed to be an example too. I'm the example of the tragic aftermath—the emotionally and mentally disturbed wreck—that someone committing suicide doesn't think about."

"Oh, Marti!"

Marti tossed her apple core into the sink and turned on the garbage disposer. "He's just trying to use me, Mom. I don't want to talk to Mr. Grant."

"Of course you don't!" her mother said. Color was returning to her cheeks, and her eyes snapped with anger. "I'm sorry, Marti. I didn't understand what he wanted. I'll tell him in no uncertain terms to leave you alone!" She stomped from the room, and Marti could hear her on the telephone in the den. She couldn't make out the words, but the tone of voice was unmistakable.

Parker Grant telephoned again an hour later, but Marti's father firmly asked him not to call the house anymore, and Grant grudgingly acceded.

Marti put him out of her mind and the next day tried to make it through classes, eager for school to be over, eager to talk to Karen again. But at noon an electric charge of excitement crackled through the high school as word got around that a film crew was on campus. Marti went into the girls' room and stayed there, ignoring the curious glances some of the girls were giving her, until the bell rang for the next period.

154

She walked out into the hallway and straight into a barrage of lights and cameras.

"I told you. There she is!" a girl called out, and Parker Grant stepped forward with a microphone.

"Marti Lewis," he said, "you were close to Barry Logan. Girlfriend? In love with him? We're told that the pain you're left with is so strong that you can't come to terms with the reality of Barry's suicide. Could you tell us how you feel about—"

With all her strength, Marti swung her shoulder bag into the microphone, knocking it to the ground. She shoved Mr. Grant as he bent to retrieve it, elbowed and pushed through the crowd that had gathered, and ran down the hall and into Mr. Thompson's empty classroom. She dropped into the nearest chair, shaking with anger, too hurt to cry.

The door opened, and Emmet came in. She was surprised when he sat next to her. "Why didn't you tell him off?" he asked.

Marti took a long, shuddering breath. "It wouldn't do any good. He wouldn't care what I said. None of them do."

"That's because nobody believes you."

The door opened and Mr. Thompson walked to his desk. He studied Marti. "Are you all right?" he asked.

"Yes," she said.

The door opened again, and she heard the same voice. "She's in here," it said.

"Oh, please!" Marti begged, and put her hands over her face.

Mr. Thompson strode to the door, barring it with his arm. "Nobody gets in here but my students," he said.

"We have permission from your superintendent to film on campus," Marti heard Parker Grant saying.

155

"Not in my classroom," Mr. Thompson said. "Now, move, please, so my students can get past you. The second bell is going to ring in a few minutes." He went out into the hallway, shutting the door firmly. Marti could hear voices rising in anger, then subsiding.

A few of the other kids straggled into the room, and Marti began to relax.

"Do me a favor," Emmet said. He held out his lit text to show her. "This page of my book got torn. The top two lines of one of the poems is gone."

Marti glanced at it. "We haven't even gotten to that section yet."

"I don't care. I need it." He shoved a piece of notepaper and a pen onto the arm desk of her chair. "You've got time now. Just write it down for me. Okay? It's no big deal, is it?"

Marti sighed. She might as well. Class wasn't going to begin for a few minutes because half the kids were still out in the hall with the television crew. She opened her book to the page Emmet indicated.

"Right there," he said and pointed. "Just the first two lines."

Carefully, Marti wrote:

I warmed both hands before the fire of life,
It sinks, and I am ready to depart.

As she got to the last word, Emmet snatched at the paper, and the pen scratched a ragged blue line across the page. Marti looked up at him, surprised.

"It doesn't have to be neat. Besides, Mr. Thompson's ready to start class." Emmet shoved the paper into his notebook.

"How many of you read the weekend's assignment?"

Mr. Thompson began, and Marti held up her hand, trying to keep her mind on what he was saying.

He didn't call on Marti. When the last bell rang he raised his voice. "Charlie, Tony, J.B., Pete—some of the rest of you—let's give Marti a little cover. Okay?" He turned to Marti. "I don't know if the reporters and cameramen are out there or not," he said. "Just to play it safe, we'll walk you to my car and I'll give you a ride home."

"Thanks!" Marti said. The tight fist that was squeezing her stomach began to unclench.

None of the network people were in sight when Mr. Thompson opened the door. Her bodyguards took her to the faculty parking lot just the same and, after she gave him directions, Mr. Thompson drove her home.

He glanced into the rearview mirror and said, "I think we've got a cop escort. Maybe I should stick around and find out why."

Marti twisted to look at the car behind them. "It's okay," she said. "It's Karen Prescott. She's a friend of mine."

Mr. Thompson stopped his car in front of Marti's house. "Take care," he said. He had asked no questions, given no advice, and Marti was grateful.

As Mr. Thompson drove off, the marked police car pulled against the curb and Karen got out. In spite of the heat her uniform was uncreased, but she looked tired. For a moment she leaned against the car, one wrist resting on the large holster at her hip. "I saw you leave the school," she said. "I heard what happened to you during your lunch hour, so I thought I'd show up about the time class let out and stand by." She walked to the house with Marti but hesitated, remaining outside as Marti opened the front door.

"Can't you come in?" Marti asked.

"I can't. I'm on duty," Karen told her, but she made no move to leave.

"Is something wrong? What's the matter?" Marti asked.

"My boss, Sergeant Bill Nieman, gave me the word in no uncertain terms," Karen said. Her voice was soft with apology. "I'm terribly sorry, Marti. As far as the brass is concerned, there is no case to investigate. I'm supposed to back off. I was told to drop my investigation."

CHAPTER · 14

Marti clung to the door for support. "I was so sure you'd help me," she whispered.

Karen took a step forward and put a gentle hand on Marti's shoulder. She looked almost as disappointed as Marti felt. "So far we've come up with nothing concrete," she said.

"We can keep trying."

"Even if this were a legitimate departmental case of suspected murder," Karen said, "only so much time would be spent on it. When leads dry up, after two or three weeks the case is filed. It's officially open, but no one works on it. Officers are assigned to other cases."

Marti rubbed the back of her hand across her eyes and stared at Karen. "I thought the police kept working until they solved every murder case."

"Only on TV, I'm afraid."

"So sometimes murders aren't solved?"

"It's not the way we want it, but that's the way it is."

Marti rested her head against the door. "I thought I could count on you."

"Oh, Marti, you can," Karen said. "Official or not, if you find out anything that might help, give me a call. I'll listen. As long as I'm with the department, I'll help where and when I can."

Marti gasped. "Do you mean they might fire you?"

"No. Not that," Karen answered. One corner of her mouth twisted up in a wry smile. "I'm getting some pressure from another source. From Greg. He wants me back in Houston and, to be honest with you, I'm considering it."

Marti studied Karen's face. "You love him very much, don't you?"

"That's been the problem all along."

"In a way, I wish you didn't love him—if he's going to make you leave Farrington Park," Marti said.

"Some of it's your fault," Karen told her.

"Mine?"

"Yes. Remember what you said about trust? I've been giving that a lot of thought. Maybe I've been too pessimistic. Maybe I've just been trying to avoid being hurt. Whatever the reason, I haven't allowed myself to trust either Greg or myself. It's kind of funny."

"Funny?"

"Yes. That I'd get a lecture on love from a girl who could be my younger sister. In some ways I think you might be older than I am."

Marti tried to smile. "I told you when I met you that I thought you were too young." She took a step forward, suddenly fearful. "Oh, Karen, don't go yet. What about

Tony and Charlie? What if something terrible happens to them?"

"We're working only with suppositions," Karen said. "We have nothing to go on, no more leads to follow."

Marti groaned and hugged her arms close to her body. "Isn't there something we can do?"

Karen thought a minute, then said, "Go over and over every single detail, Marti. Maybe there's something you haven't thought of yet, something you've seen or heard that might give us a direction to investigate. Think hard."

"If I do come up with something, will you be here?"

Karen smiled. "I'll be around for a while."

Marti watched as Karen ran down the walk, climbed into the police car, and drove away. "I won't give up," Marti said aloud, but she had never felt so terribly alone.

When she arrived at school the next morning, Marti was met by Parker Grant and his television crew. Anguished, she stared straight ahead, ignoring his questions and biting her tongue to keep from shouting what she thought of him, as she hurried up the steps and through the main doors of the school. To her surprise, she wasn't followed inside the building.

One of the school clerks, who had been watching out of the windows that flanked the doors, gave her a friendly smile. "Thank Mr. Thompson for that," she said. "He raised so much hell about the crew disrupting classes that Mr. Billingsly told them they'd have to stay out of the building."

Marti, still unnerved, hurried to her locker, where she found Kim waiting for her.

Kim stepped forward, an artificially bright toothpaste-ad smile on her face. "Why don't we do something after school? We could go to the mall." Her voice was so filled with enthusiasm, Marti wanted to tell her that she didn't have to put on such an act. "Or if you don't want to do that," Kim went on, "we could—"

Marti interrupted. "Let's go to the mall. Have you got your car?"

Kim blinked a couple of times. "You want to?"

"Isn't that what you'd like to do?"

"You mean you'll go with me?"

"That's what I said." Marti smiled. "You were trying too hard, you know. If you chewed up scenery like that in drama class, you'd get kicked out."

Kim leaned back against the lockers and giggled. "I *was* kicked out. Remember when we were putting on *The Women* and I fell over the coffee table onstage and ruined Act Two and Mrs. Harper's teaset?"

"It would be hard to forget."

Kim looked up at Marti and said, "I thought it might help if you could get your mind off everything that's been going on. You've been awfully uptight."

"I guess I have," Marti said.

"I mean, you and that police officer—"

"She's been ordered not to do any more investigating about what happened to Barry."

Kim gave a loud sigh of relief. "I really think that's good, Marti. Sooner or later you're going to have to put all of this out of your mind."

Not until I find the answers, Marti thought. *If I have to work on my own, it's going to make it harder, but I won't give up.*

During history, when they were given time for individual research on their midterm papers, Marti put the history project aside and wrote down everything she

162

could remember that concerned Barry—all that had happened, every detail, including the crank telephone calls. Someone had taken the gun from Charlie's house. Someone had gone through the things in Barry's bedroom and taken the pictures of the Cuatros. Was it because of the photograph showing the gun? Who would the picture incriminate? Only the Cuatros.

Marti realized she must have groaned, because Kim, who was seated in the row next to her, poked her with the eraser end of a pencil and made a face, shaking her head.

First of all, who would have known the hiding place of the gun? Only the Cuatros.

Unless one of them had told someone else!

The bell buzzed loudly, and Marti jumped. As everyone pushed to leave the room, Marti elbowed through the crowd until she reached Tony and grabbed his arm, jerking him to one side of the hallway.

"What's the matter with you?" Tony asked.

"Did you ever tell anyone—anyone at all—about the gun and where it was?"

Tony's eyes widened. "Keep it down. Of course I didn't. I never talked about it to anybody."

"How about Charlie? Or would you know?"

"I know. He swore to me that no one but the Cuatros knew about it."

"Do you think that Barry told anyone?"

"Never. Barry didn't even want to think about the gun." He paused. "If he told anybody, it would have been you, wouldn't it?"

So that leaves Thad.

"Are you okay?" Tony asked. "You look kind of funny."

"I'm all right," Marti said, and without another word to Tony, hurried down the hall to the girls' room. She leaned on the sink and stared at herself in the mirror, trying to think.

If Thad had talked, whom would he have talked to? The answer was obvious. To Emmet.

Barry knew Emmet. He would have let him into his house without question. Had Barry turned his back? Had Emmet struck, knocking Barry unconscious, then placed the gun in Barry's right hand and—

But how about the note? How did Emmet get Barry to write what everyone thought was a suicide note? There was no time to work that problem out now. She was going to be late for class.

By the time she arrived in Mr. Thompson's lit class, Marti's head ached. If Emmet had the answer, how was she going to discover it?

She paused in the open doorway. Most of the seats were filled. Charlie sat at the far end of the horseshoe of chairs. Tony sat in the middle of the loop next to Emmet. As Marti watched, Emmet—his back to her—pulled a piece of paper from his notebook and handed it to Tony.

What was that all about?

There was one way to find out. Debbie was sitting on Emmet's right, so Marti walked over to her, mumbled a few words of greeting, and turned quickly, bumping the arm of Emmet's chair. His notebook and textbooks went flying.

"Oh, I'm sorry!" Marti cried. She managed to elbow between Tony and Emmet, who had slid from his chair, scrabbling to pick up his books. She snatched the paper from Tony's hands. "What is this?" she asked.

"Some stuff Thompson gave before I came in," Tony said. "Emmet said I could copy his list."

Marty read:

I don't fear death any longer.

When the hounds of spring are on winter's traces.

There were two more quotations, but the first line was enough. She didn't have to read any further. "Don't copy this!" she whispered into Tony's ear. She shoved the paper back into his hand just as Emmet climbed back onto his chair.

Emmet scowled and said something to her, but the buzz of the second bell drowned out his words. Marti slipped into the lone empty seat just as Mr. Thompson rose from his desk and promptly began class. Marti watched as Tony, a puzzled frown on his face, handed the paper back to Emmet.

So that's how the "suicide note" was written. Emmet had given Barry a list like that, timing it so that Barry would only be able to copy the first one before the bell rang and Mr. Thompson took over. Maybe she should have let Tony copy his first line, just to see if Emmet would have pulled his list away as soon as the first sentence had been written. No. She couldn't take that chance with Tony's life.

"Marti, will you please read the first stanza of Coleridge's 'The Rime of the Ancient Mariner.' If you haven't found it yet, it's at the top of page 198."

Like those of an automaton, Marti's numb fingers fumbled to the correct page. *I've got to get in touch with Karen and tell her what I've found out. Tony is Emmet's next target!*

165

Shivering, she began to read, and she could hear her words strung out like lumps of ice:

It is an ancient Mariner,
And he stoppeth one of three.
'By thy long gray beard and glittering eye,
Now wherefore stopp'st thou me?'

We've got to warn Tony. Karen has to protect him.
"How has Coleridge chosen to open his poem?" Mr. Thompson asked.
"Umm . . . he's starting with the sailor, the Mariner . . . He's setting a—"
Wait! I kept Tony from copying it!
"Setting a what?" Mr. Thompson asked.
"Oh . . . a scene. He's beginning the story."
What about Charlie? Has Emmet gotten to him yet?
"Who are the three he stopped?"
"The three he . . . ? Oh. They're guests who are going to the wedding. Yes. Wedding guests."
I have to talk to Charlie and Tony. Right after class is over. Both of them.
Marti was aware that Mr. Thompson was studying her, even though he was now questioning one of the other students. She leaned back in her chair, the book unsteady in her shaking hands.
As soon as class was over Marti scrambled out of her chair, but Mr. Thompson said, "Marti, I'd like to discuss something with you, if you wouldn't mind staying. It won't take long."
"All right. In just a minute," Marti answered, but she grabbed Charlie's arm, and tried to tug him out of earshot of the others. "Did Emmet ever ask you to copy something for him?"

166

"No," Charlie said. "Why should he?"

"Marti?" Mr. Thompson called.

"Just a second," she said.

Tony joined them. "What was all that stuff you were doing before class started? I never did get those quotes we have to look up."

"Marti," Mr. Thompson said again.

"Both of you, listen to me," she whispered. "If Emmet asks you to write anything, don't do it. I'll explain later." To Tony she added, "Forget Emmet's list. We don't have to look up anything."

"Then, what—"

She began to turn, then remembered something else. "Does either of you know if Emmet has a car?" she asked.

Tony nodded. "His parents bought him one the year he got his driver's license."

"What kind is it? What does it look like?"

"I'm not sure. Ford sedan, I think. Light gray."

"It had to be," Marti murmured to herself. She walked to Mr. Thompson's desk and took the seat beside it. She saw Charlie glance back at her with such a puzzled, disturbed expression that it frightened her. *He thinks I'm crazy,* she thought.

Mr. Thompson tapped a pencil on the desk and abruptly asked, "I'll get right to the point, Marti. Are you getting any kind of counseling?"

"No," she said.

"I hope you won't object if I call your parents and suggest that they find a reputable counselor or psychologist for you."

The ache in her chest grew almost unbearable as she saw the concern in Mr. Thompson's eyes. "Do you think I'm crazy too?" she murmured.

167

"Of course not," he answered. "I think you've had more sorrow and stress than you can handle. Wouldn't you like someone to help you work through it?"

She let out a long sigh. "Yes, I would," she said. *When all this is over.*

"Then you won't object if I call your parents?"

"You can call them. They'll agree with you."

Mr. Thompson got to his feet. He looked relieved. "How about a ride home again?"

"No, thanks," Marti said. "I'm going to meet Kim. I promised to go to the mall with her."

He smiled. "That's a place I try to avoid as much as possible, especially the section around the video store. I'm too old for all that blaring music."

Her mouth opened as the thought zapped her mind. *The video store. It's where all the kids go to get records and tapes. It was probably where Emmet would have gone to buy* Sudden Death. *A copy for Barry, one for Tony, and one for Charlie. Three tapes of* Sudden Death.

Marti became aware that Mr. Thompson and she were walking out of the classrom. He was laughing and saying, "You don't have to look at me like that. I'm not that old."

"I-I know you're not," she stammered. "I just-just thought of something else." As Mr. Thompson turned to lock his door, Marti ran down the hall, where Kim was patiently waiting by their lockers.

"Hi," Kim said. "Are you ready to go?"

Marti didn't answer the question. "Can you get me last year's yearbook?" she asked.

"I've got one at home," Kim said. "So do you. What's this all about?"

"I need a yearbook right this minute. Can you take one from the yearbook office?"

Kim shrugged. "I guess."

Marti tugged at Kim's arm. "Then let's get it—now."

"I thought we were going to the mall."

"We are. As soon as I get a copy of the yearbook."

"Why do you—"

"Please, Kim," Marti said, "don't ask questions now. I'll tell you everything in a little while. Okay?"

"Well—okay," Kim answered reluctantly as Marti led her down the hall.

The yearbook office was still open, with no one around to question why Kim was taking the copy; and as soon as they arrived at the mall, Marti insisted that they had to go to the video store first.

The store was just as noisy as Mr. Thompson had said it was, and it was already filled with kids.

"I think I'm going to get that new Cyndi Lauper album," Kim said. "Let's go look at it."

"You go," Marti told her. "I'll be with you in just a minute. I have to ask the man behind the counter something."

She knew this balding, overweight man was the owner of the store, and she had never seen him leave his post behind the checkout counter. He'd probably be the only one in the store who could answer her question. As soon as he had rung up a sale and there were no other customers at the counter, Marti approached him.

"Could you tell me about any of your customers who've bought videotapes of *Sudden Death?*"

"We've sold lots of tapes and records of *Sudden Death,*" he said, his face screwing into a look of disgust. "Why, I don't know."

"Could you remember who bought them?"

169

"Are you kidding? How could I remember all those customers?"

"Would you remember someone who bought three copies of the videotape at the same time?"

"At the same time?" His eyes were narrow slits as he thought. "Well, yeah. I guess. About three or four weeks ago. There was a kid who bought three of the tapes. Said they were for friends."

"Do you remember what he looked like?"

There was a long pause while he tried to remember. Finally, he said, "I dunno. Kind of thin, I think. I'm not sure."

Marti fumbled through the yearbook until she came to the page with Emmet's picture. "Was it one of these people?"

The owner put on his glasses and bent over to peer at the page. "Yeah," he said, putting his finger under Emmet's picture. "It was him."

"Thanks." Marti snatched up the yearbook, her heart pounding in her ears, and hurried to Kim. "I have to make a phone call," she said.

"What are you doing?" Kim frowned. "I saw you showing the yearbook to the store owner. What's this all about?"

"Please trust me," Marti said. "I have to make a phone call, and then I'll need you to take me home."

"I thought we were going to have fun this afternoon. You promised—"

"Please," Marti begged.

Kim put back the album she was holding and, without another word, walked out of the store.

"Don't be angry," Marti said, following her. "This is something I have to do."

Kim leaned against the wall, her arms folded tightly. "I don't understand you anymore," she mumbled.

"If you'd just . . ." Marti stopped. She didn't have time to explain. She ran to the pay phones, dropped in some change, and asked the operator to connect her with the Farrington Park police station.

"I have to speak to Karen Prescott," she told the officer who answered.

"Officer Prescott's on duty," the man said.

"This is terribly important," Marti told him. "Do you know where she is?"

"Matter of fact, I do," he said. "She's over at I-10 helping direct traffic around an eighteen-wheeler that jackknifed and closed down three lanes."

"When can I talk to her?"

"Why don't you leave a message?" he asked. "As soon as she calls in, I'll give it to her."

"Okay," Marti said. "Please tell her that I have the proof. It's Emmet's gray car. It's Emmet who bought the videotapes."

"Hold on," he said. "I'm getting this down."

"I'm going right home," Marti said. "Ask her if she can come there as soon as possible."

"What's the address?"

"She knows it."

"What's your name?"

"Name? Oh, it's Marti Lewis."

There was a pause and his voice became brusque. "When she's free," he said, "I'll tell her you called."

"Please tell her!" Marti cried. She heard him hang up, and she leaned her head against the wall phone. *What if he didn't give Karen the message?* Marti wondered if she should just go to the station and wait for Karen.

No. She couldn't sit there for an hour or so under

171

disapproving eyes. She'd wait for Karen at home. Later, if she didn't hear from Karen, she'd try calling the station again.

She walked toward Kim, hating the closed-away look on her friend's face. "Could we go home now?" she asked.

"Why not?" Kim said, and walked as quickly as she could to her car in the parking lot, Marti meekly keeping a step or two behind her.

It wasn't until they pulled up in front of Marti's house that Kim spoke. She turned to Marti, and there were tears in her voice. "I'm not being a very good friend," she said. "I want to help you, but I've been wanting you to do things my way. I'm sorry, Marti. I'm not angry anymore. Honest. Want me to come in with you?"

"No, thanks," Marti said.

"But something's bothering you. Don't you want to have someone with you?"

Marti sighed. "Yes, but not right now. There are things I have to work out."

"Can't you tell me about them?"

"No. Not yet."

Kim shook her head in frustration. "Why not?"

Marti fought against the tears that burned her eyes. "Oh, Kim, don't you see? I don't want you to get involved in this. I don't want you to be in any danger."

Kim couldn't disguise the flash of horror that momentarily distorted her face.

She thinks I'm over the edge, Marti thought. She watched Kim struggle to disguise her feelings and cried out, "Please, Kim, trust me. I'll call you later. I'll tell you everything."

"Okay," Kim said, unable to keep her voice steady. "Why don't you do that. I'll be home. I'll be waiting."

172

"Thanks," Marti said. She picked up her books, climbed out of the car, and ran up the walk to her house, unlocking the door.

As she paused, reluctantly watching Kim drive away, she suddenly noticed that a gray car was parked halfway down the block. Marti ran a couple of steps down the walk, shouting, "Kim!" But Kim's car was already turning the corner. Kim hadn't heard her.

As she rushed into her house and shut the door, Marti wished with all her heart that her parents had listened to her, that they had installed dead bolts. Knowing how easy it was to break into this house, she felt so terribly unprotected.

She put her books on the hall table and stood silently, aware of the small noises of the house as it stirred and settled around her. She wouldn't allow herself to be afraid. Karen would call soon—surely she would. Marti would tell her what she had discovered and how she had postponed, at least, Emmet's plan for Tony.

Shivering, Marti wondered if Emmet had used the same line on Barry: You can copy this list. Maybe he had tried something different, something just as diabolical. At least Barry had been the only one to write something, at Emmet's request, that could pass as a suicide note.

Into her mind came the scene in English lit, with Emmet holding out his torn textbook: You've got time now, Marti. Write it down for me. Just the first two lines.

Marti gasped and held on to the table for support. Tony wasn't the next target. Neither was Charlie. She looked into the hall mirror at the girl with terrified eyes, whose face was as pale as her cloud of hair, and whispered, "Emmet's next victim is supposed to be *me!*"

173

CHAPTER • 15

Karen! She'd have to reach Karen as fast as possible!

The telephone in the den was the nearest one, so Marti made a dash for it, stumbling into the room, banging her leg against the coffee table as she stopped short, staring at the television set.

The picture was on, but the sound had been turned off. And the red lights of the VCR were on. Who had turned on the VCR?

Marti let out a cry as she recognized the wild gyrations of the musicians on the tape. This was *Sudden Death*!

Maybe a light sound or shadow suddenly alerted her. Marti didn't know. Overwhelmed by a wild panic, she flung herself to one side. She landed on the sofa and rolled as the poker from the fireplace came crashing down on the spot where she had been standing.

She crouched, facing Emmet, who was on his hands and knees, carried down by the force of his blow. "I'm not going to let you kill me!" she cried out.

As he rose, poker held high, Marti scrambled to her feet and grabbed the large brass table-lamp, jerking its cord from the wall, holding it out as a shield.

Tensely they waited, studying each other. "Why did you kill Barry?" she asked. "What did he ever do to you?"

"What did he do to my brother?" Emmet snarled. "The Cuatros sent him to prison."

"Thad sent himself. He's the one who robbed the store."

"They should have stuck by him. They were traitors."

His eyes glittering with anger and hatred, Emmet took a step forward. Marti stepped back, her shoulders striking the wall. "Does Thad know what you've done?"

"No," he said, "and he doesn't need to know."

"He'll find out. Everyone will."

Emmet chuckled. "They'll believe what they want to believe. You've already found that out, haven't you?" He moved a little closer.

"Listen to me, Emmet," Marti said, trying to keep her voice steady, "no matter how angry you feel, killing doesn't do any good."

"Of course it does," he said. "It's the perfect revenge."

Marti couldn't budge. The wall was against her back, the sofa on one side, the table with the telephone on the other. "If you hit me with that poker, the police will know it wasn't suicide."

"I'll take care of that. They'll never see the marks. I've got plans."

"What plans?"

"Nothing you need to know."

The telephone rang, and she involuntarily reached out toward it, but Emmet snapped, "Don't touch that!"

Afraid not to obey him, terrified of what he might do next, Marti waited through the rings until the phone was silent. Could that have been Karen?

"Copycat suicides," Emmet said. "It fits the theory so well. Barry and you and Tony and Charlie."

"Listen to me, Emmet," Marti pleaded.

"Nobody listens to you, Marti. Nobody. Dr. Granberry will be on television again, and Dr. Emery will have more ammunition for his crusade. Poor Flesh. They may be put out of business." He laughed again.

Softly the house clicked and popped as though it were disturbed. Emmet paused, listening intently. Marti could smell the sourness of her own fear, and it was hard to breathe. Maybe this was her chance, her only chance.

"Someone's in the house. Someone's coming," she whispered.

"No, they're not," Emmet mumbled, but for just an instant his glance flicked toward the doorway, away from Marti.

In that second Marti screamed at the top of her lungs and raised the heavy brass lamp. She leapt forward, whacking at the poker with the solid end of the lamp.

Emmet shouted in pain as the poker fell from his hand. But he grabbed Marti around the neck and kicked out, trying to knock her off-balance. The lamp flew to one side.

He was stronger than she had thought. His arm pressed hard against her throat, forcing her head back while she struggled. She stomped with the heel of her shoe on the top of his foot, bringing it down as hard as she could. She felt something in his foot crack as he screamed in pain.

She had pulled against him with such force that when he suddenly released her she flew forward, falling against one of the chairs and landing facedown on the floor. Crying out, she tried to rise to her hands and knees and scramble away from him as he limped toward her.

But he had the poker again, raising it high.

Again Marti rolled, and she heard the poker crash against the edge of the coffee table.

The lamp. She dove for it and swung it up just as the poker came down again. The loud clang of the metal reverberated inside her head.

She jumped to her feet and faced Emmet. He lifted the poker over his head. In an instant he'd bring it down again. The lamp was her only protection, but it would deflect the blows just so long. Marti knew she had to take a wild chance and try not just to defend herself but to stop Emmet. She suddenly twisted as though the lamp were a baseball bat. She swung it up and sideways, leaving herself completely vulnerable. Emmet's eyes gleamed, and he grinned as he aimed the poker at her head. But Marti leapt to one side, staggering off-balance as, with all her strength, she slammed the lamp into Emmet's ribs. The poker merely stung as it slid against her left arm.

Emmet collapsed into a heap, choking and moaning and sobbing. Marti snatched up the poker and lamp and dropped them next to the telephone. Crying, as the terror that consumed her rushed like ice water through her trembling arms and legs, she dialed the Farrington Park police station and in a rush of words asked for help.

"Don't break the connection," a voice said. "Someone's on the way."

She waited, afraid to leave the telephone, afraid to move closer to Emmet, until she heard a familiar voice saying, "It's all right, Marti."

Marti focused on two uniformed officers who were suddenly inside the room. One of them bent to Emmet. The one who came toward her was Karen.

"Stop shaking. You're all right now," Karen told her. She put an arm around Marti's shoulders, and Marti leaned against her.

"I didn't want to hurt Emmet," Marti whispered. "But he was trying to kill me. I had to stop him."

The officer who was kneeling beside Emmet looked up. "We'll get the paramedics," he said. "He's going to be okay."

"I know how Emmet got Barry to write the suicide note," Marti told Karen. "He was going to kill the other Cuatros too, and he told me that—"

"Take it easy. You can make a statement later," Karen said.

The telephone rang, and Marti reached for it.

"Oh, there you are," her mother said. "I called just a few minutes ago, but you hadn't come home yet." Her voice changed, a hopeful, pleading note entering it. "Your English teacher, Mr. Thompson, called me, dear. He's quite concerned about you. He feels you should get therapy. I told him that we'd discussed it. I hope you—"

The sound of her mother's voice helped everything return to normal. Marti took a long, deep breath. "Sure, Mom. I'd like to go for counseling," she said. "We can find someone, and I'll start right away."

"Oh, Marti! I'm glad, dear. I tell you what—you just

179

rest, maybe take a nap, and when your father and I get home we'll all go out to dinner. Would you like that?"

Marti watched a second pair of uniformed officers enter the room. They spoke in low voices with Karen, who gestured at the poker and the mangled shade on the brass lamp. "Sure," Marti said, "but dinner will probably be late. I've got to help fill out some reports and make a statement. You see, Mom, a little while ago—"

"Just a minute," her mother said, and Marti could hear her telling someone. "We covered that in the meeting this morning. I'll give you my notes. No. Tell him I'll be with him in a couple of minutes." She spoke into the phone again. "That's a good idea, Marti. Get your homework out of the way. I'll see you soon. 'Bye."

"Good-bye, Mom," Marti said, and hung up the phone. She turned to Karen. "Does anyone ever listen?"

"You did," Karen said, "and so did I. And I'll listen some more while the police photographers do their work in here. Let's go to the kitchen. Have you got any more diet cola?"

As Marti walked to the kitchen with Karen she glanced through the window toward Barry's house. The loneliness and sorrow were still with her, but they were softer, as though they had shed their jagged edges. *It's over now, Barry,* she thought. *I made it come out all right for you.* She took two cans of cola from the refrigerator and sat at the table across from Karen. "Okay," she said, "where do you want me to start?"

Joan Lowery Nixon

Joan Lowery Nixon is the author of more than sixty books for young readers, including *The Kidnapping of Christina Lattimore, The Séance,* and *The Other Side of Dark,* all winners of the Edgar Allan Poe Award given by the Mystery Writers of America.

Ms. Nixon lives in Houston with her husband.